THE CASE

OF THE

HOMELESS PUP

Praise for The Paul Manziuk & Jacquie Ryan Mysteries

Shaded Light: The Case of the Tactless Trophy Wife

"Ontario police detectives Paul Manziuk and his new partner, Jacqueline Ryan, make an odd team—he's white, an abrupt, patronizing veteran, while she's a recently promoted, vivacious black woman—but…the two rub elbows and tempers to captivating effect…"

Publishers Weekly

"Detailed characterization, surprising relationships, and nefarious plot-twists provide ample diversion… Recommended."

Library Journal

"A recipe for murder and mystery that simmers slowly and emits an enticing aroma reminiscent of earlier delights…"

The Charlotte Austin Review Ltd.

"Reminiscent of the best Agatha Christie had to offer… You have humor, complications, and characters so real that you can just about touch them and smell their sweat."

Midwest Book Review

Glitter of Diamonds: The Case of the Reckless Radio Host

"A master of plotting, [she] seeds her tale with concealed clues and innuendoes that keep readers guessing until the very end."

Library Journal

"The writing has humour, the story-telling is edged with compassion, and the characters are well drawn. The story is baseball, the language is the stress, ego and entertainment of professional sport and the result is an exciting stand-up triple."

The Hamilton Spectator

"The investigation is fascinating to watch as the police follow the clues and eliminate suspects one by one… An exciting baseball whodunit."

Midwest Book Reviews

"A modern-day whodunit, much in the style of the classic Christie novels.… I had to stay up all night to finish it."

Armchair Interviews

"Baseball. There are few things that say lazy, hazy summer days than that sport. But this book is anything but lazy or hazy—and is one hell of a read. A Christie-style mystery, this one does a good job of it."

Mysterical-E

Shadow of a Butterfly The Case of the Harmless Old Woman

"The characters are well etched and the vivid description of the settings gave me a feeling of actually being in the Serenity Suites where the story unfolds. I loved this book and would recommend it to all the mystery lovers."

Femme Time

"In typical Golden-Age mystery style, J.A. Menzies creates a tapestry of well-formed characters whose interplay offers—and masks—motive and opportunity for murder."

Janet Sketchley

"J.A. Menzies has become one of my favorite authors. Her characters are interesting, her plots are intricate, and her books are hard to put down… Really, I'm too old to stay awake until 3:30 am! I really, really like this book. I was sorry when it ended."

JeanBooklover

"J.A. Menzies did not disappoint! From her quirky characters to a well developed plot, I was hooked from the beginning."

Theresa Goldrick

THE CASE OF THE HOMELESS PUP

A Paul Manziuk & Jacquie Ryan NOVELLA

J. A. MENZIES

MurderWillOut Mysteries

Markham, Ontario

MurderWillOut Mysteries is an imprint of
That's Life! Communications
Box 77001 Markham, ON L3P 0C8
Email: connect@thatslifecommunications.com
http://www.murderwillout.com

DEDICATION

For anyone who's had a loved one go missing,
even for a short time. You're not alone.

ONE

Twenty minutes into his run through the woods on Tuesday morning, Evan McEwan spotted a small animal at the side of the trail ahead of him. He slowed to a stop, then moved forward as quietly as possible, squinting. What species of animal was it? A large rabbit? Coyote pup? No, it was a dog—probably a puppy—with short greyish-blond fur. Undetermined breed. Likely a mongrel. No collar.

Evan called softly, "Come here. I won't hurt you." But the puppy scampered into the trees. Evan followed, slipping quietly through the brush.

The Don River and its valley have cut a wide swath through the centre of the metropolis of Toronto. Since the river itself is now quite narrow, the valley predominately consists of trees, brush, and creeks crisscrossed by numerous trails for biking, jogging, or dog-walking. A fifth-year student at Ontario Veterinary College in Guelph, Evan was working at a vet clinic on Bayview Avenue for the summer. Since the clinic was about ten minutes west of the point at which Bayview curved to enter the Don Valley, he had decided to run the trails early in the morning before work.

At 6:40 on this particular August morning, the weather was perfect. Warm, but not too warm. Sunny, but with some cloud cover. And low humidity, which meant that when you did sweat, it would evaporate.

Evan stayed on the dog's trail for about five minutes before losing it. Then he wandered about, hoping to spot the small animal. Fifteen minutes later, as he was beginning to wonder if this was a good use of his time, he saw movement about thirty feet off to his left. After another ten minutes, he spotted the pup in a small clearing on the edge of a ravine with a narrow creek running down the middle.

In the distance was a high cliff with houses crouching along the top. Most likely estates, he thought. Anything that backed onto parkland was expensive. The cliff was so steep it wasn't likely climbed very often, but a few of the houses had zigzag stairways leading down. A wire fence in the distance separated the wooded area from the bottom of the cliff, which meant the dog might be trapped in this area trying to get home, if home was up on the cliff.

Inch by inch, Evan eased closer. When he thought the puppy should be just able to see him, he sat on the ground and remained still. Every so often, he yawned.

After a couple of minutes, he felt in his pockets and found a crumpled potato chip bag with a few chips left in it. He made a show of opening the bag and dropping a few of the chips on the ground.

The pup watched him closely, but didn't move.

It occurred to Evan that the dog might not be alone. There could be a mother dog around. Maybe another pup.

Without moving, he began to scan the area, looking for signs of other dogs peering out from behind the trees and brush. But his eyes were caught almost immediately by something on the ground just a few feet from the dog. He squinted in disbelief. Was that really a skull? Had the dog's mother died and the puppy stayed with the body? Or had the dog been walking with its owner and the owner had died? Nah. It would take weeks, if not months, for the bones to be picked so clean.

Evan cautiously pulled his cell phone from his pocket and took a picture of the dog, then one with the dog and the skull. Finally, he took a picture of the skull alone. He hit edit and cropped around it. In his studies, he'd examined a lot of different animal skulls, and he was positive this one was human.

After a moment's debate, he punched 911 and gave the person who responded the bare details of what he'd found. When questioned, he texted his location and attached the picture of the skull.

He was told to stay where he was and not move an inch until the police arrived.

The pup sat watching him, but although Evan tried everything he knew to coax it to come closer, it didn't budge until the police arrived. Then it scampered off through the trees.

The first responders took Evan through his story about how he'd found the dog and then the skull. After that, they let him phone the clinic to inform them he'd be late for work. Then they bundled him out to a small clearing closer to the main trail, where he and one of the officers waited in silence for the Forensics Identification Team, the homicide detectives, and the coroner to arrive and determine what exactly Evan had found.

Detective Inspector Paul Manziuk and Detective Constable Jacqueline Ryan were doing paperwork in Manziuk's office at police headquarters when Superintendent Seldon's call came in for Manziuk.

A tall man, easily six-foot-five, with an imposing build (in his wife's words he needed "to lose thirty or forty pounds"),

Manziuk intimidated most people at first sight—a reality he found useful most of the time.

After listening to his boss, Manziuk looked over at the young woman who had recently become his partner on the Homicide Squad. She was five-foot-nine—tall for a woman, perhaps, but nowhere near able to look him in the eye—slim but wiry, with cinnamon coloured skin, very short black curly hair, and a no-nonsense style. Young enough to be his daughter, she was from a culture that was very different from his own, which made communications troublesome at the best of times.

Not only that, but she'd had a chip on her shoulder since the day they met, and it seemed to him that she went out of her way to find things to disagree with him on. But, already, he couldn't imagine having anyone else as his partner.

"Seldon wants us to check in on a possible homicide. It's a little different." He gave her the details.

Ryan's expressive face offered him a disgusted look. "A skull in the woods? Ew!"

She began packing up. "Sure, why not? It's a nice day, and I can't say I mind getting out of here."

Ryan pulled a navy suit jacket on over her red-and-white pinstriped T-shirt before picking up the black case that held her laptop, tablet, and cell phone, as well as other odds and ends she sometimes needed at crime scenes.

Manziuk put on a tweed sports jacket and grabbed the straw hat he wore when he was going to be outside for more than a few minutes. As much as he hated the hat, it was a necessary evil to protect the balding spot on the top of his head from the sun. He picked up his own case.

"My turn to drive," Ryan said as she led the way out of the office.

Manziuk rolled his eyes but didn't argue. The decision to take turns had resolved one of their issues. Ryan kept track.

With Manziuk giving directions and occasionally suggesting she slow down, Ryan got them to their destination in good time.

One of the first officers on the scene had found a more direct route from Bayview Avenue to the crime scene, so latecomers were able to get to the clearing much more quickly than the first responders.

After getting a look at the skull, Manziuk and Ryan waited while the photographer and videographer finished their job of getting pictures from all angles.

The coroner, Dr. Weaver, arrived just as the photographer finished up. With his slim build, rather unkempt appearance, longish red hair, and abundance of freckles, Dr. Weaver was often mistaken for a college student even though he was in his mid-thirties. When he was able to get close to the skull, Dr. Weaver became animated. "This isn't fresh," he said. "Did you say a dog was involved?"

Special Constable Irving Ford, the head of the Forensics Identification Team, had come up while Dr. Weaver was examining the skull. Like Manziuk, Ford was in his mid-forties. He was a couple of inches short of six feet, but his appearance tended to remind people of the "heavy" in old police shows. Those who knew him well, however, thought of him as a large teddy bear.

Ford pointed to the ground near the skull. "You can see a few paw prints if you look closely. The ground is too dry to get much. But we have a picture of the dog, taken by the young man who found the skull."

"How big a dog?"

"Pretty small. Likely a pup. I don't think it would be big enough to carry a skull that size very far."

Dr. Weaver nodded in excitement. "So we're probably looking for a nearby burial site. Can we talk to the young man who found it?"

An officer went to get Evan, who repeated his story of how he'd found the skull before getting out his cell phone to show his pictures to Manziuk, Ryan, Ford, and Weaver.

"Why would you spend all that time chasing after a stray dog?" Ryan asked.

"I should introduce myself," Evan said. "I'm a veterinary student. Just finished my fifth year at Guelph. I'm working for the summer as an assistant at a veterinary clinic about ten minutes from here, at Bayview and Millwood. Most mornings, I come here to run before work. When I saw what looked like a lost puppy, I wanted to help it. I tried to get it to come to me, but I wasn't successful. When I saw the skull, I knew it was more important to alert you guys than to catch the dog, although I kept trying to coax it to come to me until your people arrived and it took off again."

"What do you think?" Ford asked Weaver.

"The dog's mouth looks too small for it to do more than drag the skull a short way at a time," Dr. Weaver said. "I'd suggest we start the search in maybe a hundred-metre diameter—fanning out to fifty metres in each direction. Then enlarge the scope of the area as needed."

Weaver looked at Evan. "Do you agree?

Evan nodded. "Totally. I doubt if the pup could have moved the skull far at all. Of course, we don't *know* it moved the skull. A larger animal might have brought it here earlier and the puppy may have just happened to sit down next to it at that moment."

Ford said, "Okay, as soon as we can get the rest of our team here we'll start hunting from the location of the skull fifty metres out in all directions. I'll see if we can get a cadaver dog to help, too. If the rest of the body is near the surface, we should be able to find it today."

"What about the pup?" Evan asked. "Is it okay if I keep looking for it?"

"We don't want you in the way," Ford said. "We can just call Animal Control."

"I'm not sure they'd have the time or resources to search for a lost puppy," Evan said.

"Well—" Ford looked around "—our priority is to see if there are more human remains. But if we do see the dog, I guess we could try to catch it."

Evan shook his head. "It's already scared. If you chase it, it'll be that much harder to catch."

"What do you suggest?" Manziuk asked.

"Let me look for it outside of the area where you'll be searching. And if I don't see it, maybe I could set up a live trap with some food in it."

"A live trap?" Ryan asked.

"It's basically dog kennel with a door that can be set to close if an animal goes inside. It won't hurt him at all."

Manziuk said, "What are the chances that the dog could have rabies?"

"I didn't see any signs. Still, you don't want just anybody coming across the dog. You want somebody who knows how to deal with it. And, well, I'd like the chance to find him. He's just a scared puppy."

"It's up to you," Manziuk said to Ford.

"All right," Ford said. "You can hang around. But you'll have to stay well out of our way. And if you do catch the dog, tell us immediately."

"You bet. And if your people see it, can you let me know?"

Ford nodded.

Manziuk said, "Also, we'd very much appreciate it if you don't talk to reporters. We have officers keeping them back for now, but I'm sure they'll ask for comments when they see you leave. We'd prefer that the news about this doesn't get out from anyone except us."

"For sure."

"We'll need copies of the pictures you took," Ford said. "And I'd like to remove them so there's no chance they could be accidentally released before we're ready. You can have them back later. Plus, we'll need to check over any items you have on you before you take them away."

Evan gave Ford his cell phone. "I understand."

Manziuk and Ryan and Weaver left the scene in control of Ford and his Forensic Identification Team.

Half an hour later, Evan, cell phone in hand, resumed his search for the dog.

Three hours after that, Ryan got a text message from Ford that one of the searchers had found a finger bone. Not long after that, someone found another small bone. Then the cadaver dog found the lower jaw. Soon, they located the primary burial site.

The photographer and videographer returned to document everything.

Shortly after that, Manziuk and Ryan, as well as the coroner, returned to the site and spent some time studying the remains.

"I'd say it's at least five years old," Weaver said. "Maybe double or triple that."

Manziuk nodded. "I assume we need Dr. Wong."

"Definitely. While I find this fascinating, she's the expert."

"Who's Dr. Wong?" Ryan asked. "I don't think I've heard that name."

Dr. Weaver turned to her. "Dr. Suzy Wong is the forensic anthropologist we call in when we find something out of the ordinary, like this. She lives in Toronto but travels wherever she's needed. And she teaches all over Canada and in some other countries. I don't know where she is right now."

Fortunately, Dr. Wong was at her office in Toronto, and eager to see the skeleton. Within an hour of their call, she was at the site. A petite woman with strands of grey threaded through the long black hair she had piled on top of her head, she was dressed as if on a safari in a tan blouse, a matching skirt, and a tan Tilley hat.

Dr. Wong wandered about, studying the bones and other items that had surfaced. Among the scraps of clothing found at the primary site, Ident had isolated a polyester grey fibre from a pair of pants, remnants of brown leather shoes, and a watch with a black plastic band.

Finally, Wong held the skull in glove-covered hands, studying it, then knelt to examine the pelvis and leg bones.

"Male," she said at last. "Likely Caucasian. Between twenty and thirty-five years of age. Five-foot-nine to five-foot-eleven. Healthy. The skull is fractured in two places, near the top on the right side and toward the centre of the back. I'll need to make some tests to confirm that the fractures didn't occur post mortem, but at this point, going solely on my instincts, I'd guess they were likely the cause of death. Of course, I can't say anything definite until I examine everything more closely."

Manziuk asked, "Any idea how long the body's been here?"

"I'd guess ten years minimum." Dr. Wong looked at Ford. "We need to keep going over the ground inch by inch so we get every tiny bone, every hair, and every scrap of cloth."

Evan hadn't been as lucky as the police searchers. After talking to one of the vets at the clinic where he worked, he'd been told to take the rest of the day off; but although he spent the afternoon and early evening scouring the woods outside of the police lines, he saw nothing of the pup.

Finally, he drove to the clinic and asked if they had a large live trap he could use. Since they didn't have a lot of use for them, at first the answer was no. But one of the technicians, who'd been there for many years, remembered there had been one and found it on the top shelf of a storage room. She also found some no-spill dishes for food and water to leave in it.

Evan went back to the woods and set up the trap as close as he could get to the site where he'd found the dog. He knew he was more likely to trap a raccoon, a porcupine, or a rabbit, but it was the best he could do.

He returned the following morning before work, released the anxious rabbit he'd caught, and reset the trap. He was resigned to coming back each morning and evening for the time being.

Two days after the skeleton arrived at her laboratory, Dr. Wong sent in her report. The body was that of a young Caucasian man in his early twenties to early thirties. He had a slim build. His hair was dark brown, cut short, with a bit of a wave. The only abnormality was a break in his right tibia, likely in his teens, which had healed properly.
After a close inspection of the man's dental work, she thought he was a Canadian or possibly American citizen. She also felt that, if they could narrow down the possibilities, dental records should identify him without much difficulty.

Dr. Wong had been able to get DNA from the hair and bones, but they would need to have a family member's DNA to match.

The immediate job for the police was to go through the missing persons reports for the Greater Toronto Area for the time period between 1990 and 2010.

At seven-thirty on Thursday evening, eight hours after she and three other officers began looking through the old missing persons files, Constable Brianna Fossey walked up to Constable Ryan's desk in the Homicide Squad's main room. "I've got a possible fit for the skeleton."

"Super. Let's go to Inspector Manziuk's office."

The two women walked the short distance to the corner office, where Manziuk sat at his desk. Ryan took a position leaning against the window sill while Fossey sat on the edge of a chair.

"This is a missing persons report from October 18, 1999," Fossey said. "It's for a man named Antonio De Luca. He was 27, married, with two little kids. Tony—which is what people called him—lived in Little Italy, just south of College Avenue. He worked at Chiarelli's Barber Shop on College.

"His wife told the police that Tony normally walked to and from work unless the weather was bad. It was about a twenty-minute walk. He occasionally stopped off at a local pub on the way home. According to his boss, a man named Raphael Chiarelli, on Friday, October fifteenth, Tony left work at nine p.m." She looked up. "He was apparently the last person to see Tony."

She glanced back down at her notes. "A friend of his, Dom Marino, waited for a while at the pub where they normally met, and then went home. He assumed Tony had changed his mind.

"His wife went to bed, thinking Tony was at the bar with Dom. When she woke up Saturday morning and Tony wasn't home, she called Dom first, then Tony's boss, and then the police."

Fossey looked up again. "This is where it's kind of bad. The police officer she spoke with told her that her husband was likely taking the weekend off." She made a face. "No doubt under the 'boys will be boys' rule."

"Idiots!" Ryan said.

Manziuk shook his head in disbelief.

"When Tony didn't show up by Monday morning, his wife and his parents went to the police station and filed a missing persons report." Fossey said. "And that's it. He was never found. The last note from the investigating officers is that they thought he had chosen to disappear."

Ryan frowned. "Why would they think that?"

"Maybe I'm reading between the lines, but the impression I got is that they figured he was overwhelmed with all the responsibility from having a wife and two kids when he was only twenty-seven."

Manziuk asked, "Was the case ever reopened?"

"Two notes were added." Fossey leafed through the pages. "The first is from 2002. That year, under the Survivorship and Presumption of Death Act, his wife and parents applied for presumption of death and it was granted.

"The second note is from 2013. It says that the wife, Gina, remarried in 2005. Her second husband was Dom Marino, who was one of Tony's best friends and the person he was supposed to meet in the pub the night he disappeared. At the time of his disappearance, Tony and his wife and kids lived in the main part of his parents' house and his parents lived in the basement. Gina and the kids stayed there.

"In 2011, Tony's mother died from a heart attack.

"In 2013, Gina and Dom were still living in the main part of the house, and the father was still in the basement. Tony's two children, a daughter Felicia and a son Bruno, were aged nineteen and sixteen at that time. And Gina had two younger kids—both boys—with her new husband."

Ryan asked, "Was there any indication that the police suspected foul play?"

"The investigating officer who looked at it in 2013 seemed to suspect that was the case, but since the trail was pretty cold, and there was no body or anything to suggest where a body might be found, he shelved it."

Fossey leaned so far forward she looked as if she might fall off her chair. "But wait until you hear this! The night Tony went missing, he was wearing a grey T-shirt with white sleeves, dark grey flannel pants, and brown loafers. Plus, he had a Timex watch with a black band. Those tally with what was found, right? Also, he broke his right leg playing high school football."

"Sounds promising," Manziuk said.

"There's one other thing. Other than his wallet, which hasn't been found, he always wore a gold cross his mother gave him when he was eighteen. I don't think that's been found, has it?"

"No," Ryan said. "But the wallet and chain are the kind of things that might well have been stolen." She shrugged. "A Timex watch, maybe not so much."

"I think we need to follow this up," Manziuk said. "Thanks for spotting it, Brianna. Can you make sure Ford sees this, and can you make a copy of the file for us?"

"I'll do it right away." She left the office.

Manziuk started packing up to leave. "We need to talk to the widow. If it seems like a fit, she might be able to tell us where we can get the dental records."

Ryan had turned to look out the window.

"What are you thinking about?" Manziuk asked.

"His family. How they must have felt. To have your husband and father go to work in the morning and never come home. And never know what happened to him."

Manziuk paused. "Horrible."

"And now, how they'll feel to find out he was dead all this time."

Ryan turned. "Wouldn't you have been on homicide back then?"

"Yes, but this would have been a missing persons case. There are something like twenty thousand missing persons cases a year in Canada. Most of them are resolved within a few days or a week. Cases like this one—all too often, there's nothing to go on.

"And the chances of a missing persons case being a homicide is actually very slight. Especially a man like this, with no police record, no gang involvement, a family, and a good job. So you start wondering about other things. Depression. An affair—maybe he wanted to be with another woman but didn't want the mess of a divorce. Or maybe he just had the desire to be free from his obligations. It happens. More often than murder. I can see why they'd leave it at that when nothing else showed up."

"They must have missed something." Ryan looked at Manziuk. "So you want to talk to his widow right away?"

"Yes. If she works, she's more likely to be at home in the evening. And there's a chance she's already heard the news reports about human remains being found and is wondering. Along with everyone else whose loved one is missing. Plus, despite all our efforts to contain this, there could be a leak, and that wouldn't be good at all. We need to get at the truth and let the public know as soon as we possibly can."

"Okay. I'll pick up the file from Brianna and meet you at the car. I'll even let you drive while I go over it."

"You'll 'let' me drive?"

Manziuk was still laughing when Ryan left his office.

The home where Tony De Luca's wife still lived was a detached two-storey on a residential street south of College

Avenue, near Ossington. The house was across from a large park with mature trees, benches, and picnic tables.

The reddish-brick house was old but well-maintained. It had a raised main floor, with eight steps leading up to the door. The postage-stamp-sized front yard was nicely land-scaped with raised brick beds containing a Japanese maple tree and bright bunches of flowers. Manziuk thought the yellow ones were sunflower. There were also several orange and red coneflowers and purple chrysanthemums. He recognized them only because his wife, Loretta, had cultivated similar plants in their yard over the years.

A brick path led from the sidewalk to the front steps and wrapped around the left side of the house to another door that likely led to the father's basement suite. He knew that many of the houses in this area had basement suites with separate entrances.

Manziuk and Ryan went up the steps to the front door, and Ryan rang the doorbell.

A moment later, a young woman in black shorts and a red T-shirt opened the door and frowned. "May I help you?"

Manziuk smiled. "Would you be Felicia Marino?"

The woman, who was of medium height with dark, wavy brown hair, exchanged her frown for a puzzled look. "Yes," she said cautiously.

"Is your mother home? We'd like to speak with her."

At first, Felicia looked as if she wasn't going to admit them. Then she turned and called out, "Mom, someone for you." Looking back at them, she said, "She'll just be a minute."

The three of them waited in the doorway until an older version of Felicia appeared. Her shorts were white and her T-shirt was royal blue. "What is it? I'm not buying anything."

Manziuk said, "Gina Marino, formerly Gina De Luca?"

The woman clutched her hands to her chest. "Who—who are you?"

"We're with the police." Manziuk held out his ID.

"Oh, my Lord! You've found him, haven't you?"

Ryan took a step forward. "May we come in?"

After giving both detectives a measuring look, Felicia took her mother's arm and half-guided, half-propelled her through the tiny hallway into the adjoining sitting room on the left.

Ryan shut the front door and followed Manziuk into a rectangular room with a large front window and a smaller side window. A matching floral blue and gold brocade chesterfield, loveseat, and easy chair dominated the space. Manziuk and Ryan sat on either end of the chesterfield.

Gina Marino huddled on the edge of the loveseat with her daughter's arm around her shoulders. "Am I right? Have you found him? Is that why you're here?"

Manziuk said, "Can we talk freely? Your other children…?"

Felicia replied. "My brother Bruno is out, and the younger boys are upstairs, supposedly in bed, but likely playing video games."

"Tell me," Gina said. "You can't imagine what it's been like all these years, wondering, waiting…"

Manziuk said, "Mrs. Marino, you may have heard on the news that human remains were found in a wooded area in the Don Valley a couple of days ago. We've been going through a process to determine whose remains they are. At this point, we're simply checking all possibilities. That's *all* this is. A possibility. The person whose body was found was a young man, and the time period includes the time in which your husband went missing. That's why we've come to see you. We're wondering if you remember who your husband's dentist was. If we could get the dental records, that would help us either cross him off our list or identify him."

"What about DNA?" Felicia asked. "You could test his against mine and Bruno's."

Manziuk smiled at her. "Dental records would be the fastest and easiest way if they're available. But yes, we can test the DNA if necessary."

Gina leaned toward Manziuk. "May I see him?"

Felicia pulled her mother back. "Mom, if Daddy's been in the woods for all that time, there's just bones."

"I would still like to see for myself." Gina sobbed once and brought her hands up to cover her mouth. When she'd regained her composure, she said, "I never once for even a second believed Tony left of his own free will. I always knew he was either dead or being held against his will some place. I hoped he was dead, because the other was too terrible to even consider."

"Mrs. Marino," Ryan said, "do you have pictures of your husband? We have the one that was given to the police when he went missing, but I'm wondering if you have others."

Gina sat up straighter. "Of course. Felicia, get the brown album."

Felicia crossed the room to pull a photo album from a low bookcase beneath the side window. As she walked back, she said, "Why don't we go into the dining room? You'll be able to look at it more easily."

TWO

The room on the other side of the front entranceway was crowded with a large walnut dining room table, eight chairs, and a huge buffet.

Gina took a chair in the middle of the table on one side, with Manziuk and Ryan on either side of her. Felicia sat at the end next to Ryan.

Gina flipped to the back of the album and showed them photos of Tony in the last year before he disappeared.

In one of the pictures, Tony was wearing a white T-shirt with grey three-quarter-length sleeves, dark grey pants, and brown loafers. Ryan pointed at it. "That looks like what the report said he was wearing on the day he disappeared."

"Yes, it was."

"Do you by any chance remember exactly what kind of watch he had on?"

Gina nodded. "I remember perfectly. It was a Timex Ironman Triathlon. I bought it for his birthday the month before. He told me what kind he wanted. It had all kinds of gizmos and you could wear it in water. He loved it." Tears welled up again.

"Mama," Felicia said, "you told me he always wore a gold chain with a cross."

"Yes, he did. His mother gave it to him when he was eighteen, and he only took it off to shower. And not always then."

Felicia looked from Ryan to Manziuk. "Did you find the watch or the chain?"

Manziuk cleared his throat. "All I can say at this point is that we did find a few articles of clothing and other items, but they're not in very good condition. We're studying them."

"His wallet?" Felicia asked.

"So far, there's been no sign of a wallet or any form of identification."

"So it could have been robbery?"

"It could."

Felicia frowned. "But you said the remains were found in the Don Valley? How could his body get to the woods miles and miles away from the barber shop?"

Manziuk said, "Please remember, we're only at the beginning of our investigation, and we don't yet know if this is your father's body."

"Yes, I realize that. But as you can imagine, I'm very curious. I was six years old when my father disappeared. I remember him. And something like that is just as devastating for a young child as it is for an adult. Maybe more so because to a child the loss can be incomprehensible."

"Our dentist is Dr. Pierno," Gina said suddenly. "I don't know if he kept Tony's records or not, but he was our dentist back then, too. He has an office on College Street. I don't remember the number, but I can find it."

Felicia said, "I have it in my phone." She quickly gave Ryan the number.

"Thank you," Manziuk said. "We'll check with him. Now, is your husband's father still living?"

"Yes, but he's not in right now. He usually goes for a drink with friends in the evening. He should be back by ten or ten-thirty. They never stay out late."

"Do you think it would be best for us to tell him about the investigation, or would you prefer to tell him yourself?"

"I need to tell Dom—my husband—first. Then—" Gina took a few deep breaths. "Maybe it would be best coming from you. He might have questions. Dom was Tony's best friend. They were like brothers. I'm sure he'll want to talk to you himself."

"Where would we find your husband?"

"He had to work late tonight. He's at his office. He's in real estate. On Dundas, not far from here. If you went there, when you come back, Tony's father should be at home. He lives in our basement but he has his own entrance on the side of the house."

Manziuk and Ryan stood up to leave.

Felicia stood, too. "Can I visit the place where you found the body?"

Ryan said, "Do you mean the location in the woods?"

"Yes."

"I guess so," Ryan said, "but there's crime scene tape around the area where the remains were found, so don't cross it. But you can go up to it if you want. If you'll give me your email address, I'll send you directions for getting there."

"Thank you." Felicia shrugged and smiled. "I realize this might not be him, but I don't think you'd be here if you didn't have a good reason, so I want to know as much as possible. You can ask anyone who knows me—I hate being kept in the dark about anything."

Ryan smiled back. "I can definitely relate to that."

The front door of Marino Real Estate's small street-side office was open, and the receptionist's outer desk empty, but a slim man with curly black hair came out of an inner office moments after Manziuk and Ryan walked through the front door. He wore navy suit pants, a tan short-sleeved shirt, and a big smile. "Good evening. How can I help you people? Are you looking for a new house?"

They gave him their names and showed him their I.D. "Are you Dominic Marino?" Manziuk asked.

His face took on a puzzled look, but the smile remained. He held out his hand and nodded. "Just call me Dom, officers. To what do I owe this pleasure?"

After suggesting that they all sit down in his office, Manziuk explained their visit to Gina.

For a long moment, Dom sat looking out the window to the side of his desk. Then he turned back to them. "This is a huge shock. I—well, it's been so long. Sixteen, no, seventeen years. Not that we've ever forgotten Tony. It's just—you get used to things the way they are. So this—this is a tremendous shock. But not a surprise, if you understand. I'm sure Gina told you we—none of us—believe that he left by choice. Unless—I have to confess that I did finally become reconciled to the idea that he'd been depressed and went away to commit suicide. That there was something going on that none of us knew about, and that he'd just gone away to a lake up north and drowned himself or something like that. And that's why his body was never be found. That's the only thing that made any sense to me. But I never thought of anything like this."

He took a deep breath, and it was as if new energy surged into his body. "How positive are you that this body you've found is Tony's?"

Manziuk said, "We aren't certain at all. At this point, we're simply following up possibilities."

"Do you need somebody to identify the body?"

"Well, at this point, it's not that simple."

"Oh, of course. I—I wasn't thinking. So what do you do?"

"We're going to start by comparing dental records."

"So teeth are one of the things that don't—what is the word they use—decompose?"

"Yes, unlike skin and other organs, teeth stay around for a long time."

"And bones, I guess."

"Yes."

Dom took another deep breath. "Well, I'll leave you to it then. And I'd better get home." He gave them a wry smile. "I don't think I'll get any more work done today."

As he walked with Manziuk and Ryan to the front door, Dom asked, "Did you happen to meet Felicia?"

Ryan said, "Yes, she was at the house."

"I'll bet she had a million questions."

"She seemed very interested. She would have been really young when he disappeared, but she remembers him."

"I think maybe his disappearance was a big reason why she ended up in psychology. Wanting to understand how people think, and why they do what they do." Dom grinned. "She watches all the cop shows, too. I expect she'll keep you on your toes."

While Manziuk drove back to the house, Ryan made some calls. After a few minutes, she had the home phone number for Dr. Alonzo Pierno. She phoned him and explained their situation.

"You're looking for the dental records for Tony De Luca?"

"That's right. Any chance you would still have them? And if so, would there be an X-ray?"

"As a matter of fact, there's a very good chance. I never believed anything but the worst about Tony's disappearance. When they didn't find his body right away, I said to myself,

'You hold onto this folder because one of these days they're going to find him and this will be important.' I'll be at my office by seven in the morning. Is that soon enough for you?"

"We'll send an officer to pick it up."

"It'll be ready. And no, I won't say anything to anybody about this. Not even my receptionist."

"Thank you for understanding."

"No need to thank me. I liked Tony De Luca. The whole De Luca family for that matter. I want you to catch whoever did this and make him pay."

Manziuk and Ryan waited outside the Marino house until they saw an older man come down the sidewalk and turn into the walkway, then turn left and continue along the side of the house. It was 10:15. They waited a few more minutes to let him get inside.

There was an intercom next to the side door, and when Manziuk rang the bell, a male voice asked who it was.

"Detective Inspector Paul Manziuk and Detective Constable Ryan. May we speak with you for a few minutes, please?"

"You're cops?" came the crusty voice.

"Yes. We've already spoken with your daughter-in-law, and she told us when you'd be home."

There was a buzzing sound, and Ryan opened the door. They went down the steps to the basement apartment.

Mario De Luca met them at the foot of the stairs. He was a slightly stooped man with a good head of black hair that was flecked liberally with grey. It was cool in the basement, and he wore a charcoal cardigan with the sleeves pushed up. His hands were on his hips and he was frowning. "What's this about?"

"Could we sit down, Mr. De Luca?"

"Mario is fine. Is this about Tony?"

"It might be. Could we sit down?"

After staring at them for a long moment, Mario led the way into what appeared to be a sort of all-purpose dining room, living room, and office. A small table in the centre had four chairs, so they sat around it.

"Nothing wrong with my heart, and I won't get hysterical," Mario said, "so just tell me what's up. I can see from your faces that it's not good news."

Manziuk explained their mission.

"So you'll be able to compare the dental records with the teeth you found?"

"We were able to phone Dr. Pierno at his residence, and we'll pick up your son's records first thing in the morning."

Mario said, "It's not an easy thing to lose your only son. Not easy at all. After it happens, no matter what anybody says, there's a part of you missing. It killed my wife. No matter what the doctors might say, she grieved for Tony for eleven years, and then she died. If this is his body, I'm glad to know. I've spent all these years wondering, not wanting to believe he was dead, but knowing he had to be. But I don't have any energy to waste. So you find out if it's him, and then come back and we'll talk about whatever comes next."

At 6:45 Friday morning, Felicia Marino stood at the edge of the crime scene tape looking at the hole in the ground where the majority of the bones had been found. She had no idea what she'd been expecting to see here. Or what she ought to be feeling.

Since the age of six, she'd been waiting for her beloved daddy to come home. Now, convinced the police wouldn't have come to their home unless they'd been ninety-nine percent positive they'd identified his body, she had to accept that he never would come home.

She ought to feel something. Relief, maybe. Because he hadn't been able to come home. He'd been lying dead the whole time. He hadn't deserted her.

But instead she felt numb. And she had so many new questions. How had he died? And why here? Had he come for a walk and had an accident? Had he committed suicide? Had he met someone here and had a disagreement? Was he doing something illegal? Or had someone killed him elsewhere and hidden the body here so it wouldn't be found?

Just knowing her dad hadn't been able to come home wasn't enough for her.

She felt rather than heard a movement behind her and whirled around. A muscular young man with ash blond hair was standing not ten feet away. He wore a sleeveless Toronto Raptors' jersey and khaki shorts.

"Sorry," he said. "I didn't realize someone was here."

Felicia's heart rate gradually slowed. The man was young—about her age—and he didn't look threatening. Still, they were in a wooded area, far from other people. She put her hand in her pocket and grasped her cell phone, ready to call 911. "Are you with the police?"

"No, I'm looking for a dog."

She frowned. "You lost your dog here?"

"Not exactly. I saw a stray dog a few days ago and followed it and found a body. But I'm still trying to catch the dog. That's my live trap over there." He pointed to an empty wire cage Felicia hadn't noticed.

But that wasn't what interested her. "*You* found the body?"

"Well, it wasn't really a body. Just the skull. And it was the dog who found it. I just happened along."

"That was probably my dad's skull you found. The police came and told us about it last night."

"Oh. I didn't realize… I'm so sorry."

"What's this about a dog? The police didn't give us details."

"It was a puppy, actually." He held out his hand. "My name's Evan, by the way."

"Felicia. Tell me about finding the body. I want to know every single detail."

"Do you have time for a coffee?"

"I was thinking breakfast. By the time I get back to the parking lot, I'm going to be starved."

Evan smiled. "Let me check my live trap, and I'm right with you."

❧

As Dr. Wong had suggested, dental records turned out to be all they needed. All four of Tony's wisdom teeth had been removed. His left front tooth had been broken in a street hockey accident and a cap put on it. And he had several other fillings that matched the fillings in the teeth belonging to the skull. When Dr. Wong superimposed the old X-ray over the photo she'd taken of the teeth in the skull, it was a perfect match.

So they had a name. Next up was to determine how Tony De Luca died.

Manziuk and Ryan conferred with Dr. Wong, Dr. Weaver, and Special Constable Ford.

They agreed that the skull fractures on the back and right side of the skull were likely the cause of death. Both fractures were consistent with the impact of a blunt object. However, there was no way to tell whether the object had hit the body or the other way around.

Tony could have tripped and fallen and hit his head. However, simply falling didn't really account for the amount of force needed to fracture the skull not once but twice. And it was inconceivable that Tony had gone to the woods by himself and fallen, died, and buried himself there.

In the end, they agreed that the most likely explanation was that Tony had died elsewhere and his body had been brought to the woods and buried about three feet below the surface. Wild animals had dug up part of the body and scattered some of the bones and fibres. Erosion and shifting earth had also played a role. Finally, a wild animal or a dog had dragged the skull some distance from the body, and the small puppy had found it and perhaps dragged it further.

The important thing for the police was that a second person had to have been involved. So Tony De Luca's death was officially ruled a homicide.

Special Constable Sam Benson was waiting in Manziuk's office when he and Ryan came back from their meeting with Wong and the coroner. An extrovert who had a natural way with words, Benson was well-suited to handling public relations so that detectives like Manziuk and Ryan could focus on solving the crimes.

Benson stood up when the door opened. "Seldon says the body in the Don Valley has been called a homicide, and you know who it is."

"That's right," Manziuk said.

"Good. I've had reporters giving me a hard time ever since they heard about the human remains being found. What can I give them?"

"You can confirm that it's now a homicide investigation, and that we have identified the body as belonging to a Toronto man, but that we can't reveal his name until the immediate family has been informed. We'll be doing that as soon as possible."

Ryan added, "Is it okay to let them know that the body has been there for some years? It's not recent."

"Yes," Manziuk said. "That's fine."

"There's a rumour going around that a dog was involved," Benson said, "and they're asking for details. Was somebody walking a dog, or what?"

Manziuk looked at Ryan. "Can you check with—Evan, isn't it?—to see if the dog has been found yet?"

While she stood up and moved to a corner of the room to make the call, Manziuk gave Benson the basic details, and then added, "I don't want this to get out yet. The last thing we need is reporters running through the woods trying to catch the dog. After we have the dog, you can give the reporters a picture and some of the details. Evan may or may not want his name included. That's up to him."

Ryan came back to her seat. "Evan hasn't found it yet, but he's still trying. I asked if he's talked to any reporters, and he said he hadn't but that several of them saw him the first day and found out his name and have been around to ask him if he knows anything. One of them apparently stopped him last night when he got out of his car to go and check the live trap."

Manziuk said to Benson, "Keep the info about the dog and how the body was found under your hat for now."

Benson made a face. "You haven't given me much of anything to work with."

Ryan grinned at him. "I'm sure you can make it seem like more than it is."

"Ha, ha."

Manziuk said, "When we have something, you'll be the first to know."

"Should I ask this guy if I can help find the dog? People like feel-good stories about dogs. Maybe if it's a stray, we can get him a good home. That would make everybody happy."

"I'll give you Evan's number," Ryan said. "Maybe you can become jogging buddies."

Benson grimaced. "What I do for you people!"

Manziuk got up and stood staring out his office window at the sidewalk three stories below. People walking past, going on about their daily lives. People just like Tony De Luca. Until his life stopped.

Ryan sat at the desk with her laptop open, waiting.

"All right," Manziuk said, without turning from the window. "Let's go over what we know from the original missing person report and the follow-up."

"According to his boss, he left work at the barber shop shortly after nine p.m. on a Friday night," Ryan said. "Gina went to bed thinking he was at a pub with his friend Dom. In the morning, she discovered he hadn't come home. After talking to his boss and Dom, she called the police. They didn't take it very seriously, especially after Gina admitted that Tony had stayed out all night a few times when he'd had too much drink." Ryan looked up. "It says Dom told her he'd waited, but Tony never showed up. That ought to have been a red flag."

"Just give me the facts. We can comment on the mistakes they made later."

"All right. Gina and Tony's father called in person Monday morning when Tony still hadn't come home and hadn't shown up for work. That's when the police began to take his disappearance seriously."

"Okay. What did they do?"

"Interviewed his family, co-workers, friends, and so forth. Everyone the officers talked to said he was well liked and had no enemies."

"What did they conclude?"

"That he'd done a runner."

Manziuk spun around. "Why?"

"He had no record, he seemed awfully young to have so many responsibilities, and they had nothing to go on."

"Did they search his house?"

"Yes. Nothing."

"Did anyone suggest another woman?"

"Not really. But there was a comment that he seemed like the kind of guy women might be attracted to."

"Any signs of depression?"

"No."

"And nothing of his was ever found?"

"Credit cards were never used. Wallet never found. He simply vanished."

"All right. Let's go over the few facts we have. His boss says he left work shortly after nine. Dom says he waited for him at the pub, but he never arrived. Gina is adamant that he never came home."

"Not much to start with."

"Did he have a cell phone?" Manziuk asked.

"No."

"All right." Manziuk began pacing around the room. "The difference between then and now is that we know he died, probably that night. So we have a starting point. We'll begin by interviewing everyone the missing persons officers talked with back then, and perhaps we can expand that list."

"Should we start by talking to the original investigating officers?"

"Who were they?"

"Sloan and Rasminsky."

Manziuk shook his head. "That won't help us. Jerry Sloan died in a car accident and Devin is in nursing home—Alzheimer's."

"Ouch."

"Afraid we're on our own. Let's start with his wife and his father. First, we need to tell them we've identified him. No doubt they'll want the remains released for burial as soon as possible."

Ryan said, "What about the wallet? It hasn't been found. Plus his wife said he always wore a gold chain with a cross."

Manziuk thought for a moment. "The obvious answer is that a thief took them. I suppose it might be worth getting a photo of the chain from Gina. We can send it to jewellers and pawn shops in the area. But I suppose it's possible a crow or an animal might have carried it off."

"The two items are still loose ends."

"Agreed."

When Manziuk and Ryan knocked on the door of Gina and Dom Marino's home, it was opened by a young man with longish, wavy, dark brown hair. A young man who immediately made Manziuk recall the photo of the dead man. "Bruno Marino?" he asked.

"That's right. Who are you?"

Manziuk made the introductions and asked for Bruno's mother.

"She's downstairs with my grandfather."

"Perhaps we'll go there, then."

"All right." Bruno shut the door.

Manziuk and Ryan went to the side door and rang the doorbell. As before, Mario De Luca's voice came over the intercom. When they gave their names, he buzzed the door open. Downstairs, they sat at the small table with Mario and Gina.

"It's him," Gina said.

"Yes," Manziuk said, "I'm afraid it is."

"Don't be sorry. It's good to know."

The old man wiped away a tear. "No, it's not good."

"Oh, Papa!" Gina's own tears began to flow. "You're right. It's not good. It's not what anyone wanted. But at least now we can bury him with Mama."

The old man turned away, his shoulders heaving, and Gina put her arms around him. "Please," she said to Manziuk. "I know you will want to talk to us more, to ask questions. But please give us a little time to grieve first."

None of them had heard Bruno come down the inside stairs from the floor above. "How did my father die?" he asked. "Did someone kill him?"

Gina immediately hustled Bruno upstairs, with Manziuk and Ryan following. She then phoned both her husband and her daughter and asked them to come home immediately. The younger children would be in school for another hour, but she arranged for a neighbour to pick them up and keep them at her house for a while. Then she went back downstairs to be with her father-in-law.

Following Bruno's vague directions, Ryan made coffee and got out some cookies; after which the three of them sat in the sitting room waiting for Dom and Felicia to arrive.

Dom was first. After learning that Tony's body had been identified, he spoke to Bruno for a few minutes and then went downstairs.

After Felicia arrived, Gina, Dom, and Mario came upstairs and everyone sat in the front room.

As succinctly as possible, Manziuk went over what they'd found and their reasons for concluding that Tony's death was a homicide.

When he finished, they were all very quiet, looking at each other but not speaking.

At last, Bruno broke the silence. "So you believe my father was murdered and his body was buried in the woods so it wouldn't be found?"

"That's our working theory."

"What will you do now?"

"At this point, we have to begin from scratch. We'll need to interview everyone who knew him back then, and try to piece together what happened. But because it happened nearly seventeen years ago, it's possible we may not be able to find all the answers we all want."

Felicia spoke. "So this is what they call a cold case?"

"Well, in one sense. But now it's a very active case."

"How can we help?"

"We'd like to ask some questions of you as a group, and then we may want to interview each of you individually."

"Now?"

"That would be ideal."

"Yes," Gina said. "I want to get it over with."

The others nodded. "If my son was murdered," Mario said, "I want the person who did it punished."

Ryan, who was sitting at the back of the room, opened her laptop.

"All right," Manziuk said. "What do you remember of that day? It was a Friday in October."

"It was just a normal day in the fall," Gina said. "Not too hot or too cold. I worked in the morning, and then I took the kids to the park after school ."

"Where did you work?"

"At a coffee shop a few blocks from here. I worked from six in the morning until two in the afternoon. But it closed a long time ago."

"So you weren't here when Tony left for work?"

"No. I often wasn't. Most days he left at eight-thirty, but when he worked the late shift, he left at eleven-thirty. So that day he would have left later."

"Where were your children during that time?"

"Tony might have helped them dress, but Mama De Luca would come up and make breakfast and lunch. And either she or Tony would take Felicia to school and the other would look after Bruno. Felicia had just started grade one that fall, so she was in school all day."

"It was Mama's greatest joy," Mario said, "looking after Tony's little ones. After he disappeared, it was her only joy."

"Did you come up at all during that day?" Manziuk asked the old man.

"I left for work at seven each weekday," he said, "until I retired five years ago."

"And your occupation?"

"I'm a carpenter. I still do odd jobs."

Manziuk turned to Gina. "So you came home from work after two, and took the children to the park?"

"Well, not right away. Bruno was still having his nap when I got home. When it was nearly time for Felicia's school to end, I got him up and we walked to meet her. Then we went to the park across the street."

"I see. So what happened next?"

"We came home and I did some housework while the kids played with their toys and watched a TV show. Then I made supper, and we ate and played a few games. I put the children to bed about eight and read them some stories. That's what happened most days. Then I watched television until I went to bed around ten."

"Was it usual for you to be in bed when Tony came home?"

"Only when he worked late on a Friday night. He'd often meet Dom and sometimes my brother Emil at a pub. Usually he'd come home around midnight. Never later than two."

"When did you realize he hadn't come home?"

"When I got up in the morning. He had Saturday off and we'd planned to take the ferry across to Centre Island that day. But when I got up, he wasn't in bed, and the covers were still pulled up and flat as if he hadn't been there. And his pillow looked unused. I went to the front room, thinking he might have slept on the couch, but he wasn't there. After I checked the bathroom, I didn't know what else to do, so I called Dom. I thought maybe if he'd had too much to drink, he might have slept at Dom's."

Manziuk turned to Dom. "And he hadn't?"

"No. Tony was supposed to meet me after the barber shop closed at nine." Dom leaned forward. "It's strange, but I remember that night as clearly as if it was last week." He coughed. "At first, I didn't realize he was late. I mean, I knew a lot of the other guys who were there, so I was talking to them. And we were all watching the Leafs playing the Chicago Blackhawks. It was probably getting on for ten when I realized Tony hadn't showed up. I just figured something had come up, or maybe he'd told me he had something on that night and I'd forgotten. After the game ended, I played some darts and I went home around eleven."

"How did you react when Mrs. De Luca phoned you the next morning?"

"I was flabbergasted. I told her to call Raphael, and then call me right back."

"Raphael?"

"Tony's boss at the barber shop," Gina said. "I called him, and he said Tony had left at about ten after nine, as usual. That's when I phoned the police. But the person I talked to didn't seem worried. He said to check the hospitals and that it was most likely Tony had pulled an all-nighter—whatever that means. I told him Tony wouldn't do that, but he said something about wives being the last to know and hung up."

"So you phoned the hospitals?"

"No. I called Dom, and he said he would. I—I just— Felicia and Bruno were up by then and I didn't want to be doing that in front of them. And I didn't want to worry Papa and Mama De Luca."

Manziuk looked at Dom. "You phoned the hospitals?"

"Yes. I even phoned the morgue. Then I went over and talked to Raphael. I thought between the two of us we'd be able to figure out where Tony might have gone. But Raphael was busy with customers, and he had no suggestions. So I walked from the barber shop to the bar, the same way Tony would have walked, looking for anything that might be a clue, you know? Like a place he might have stopped in or something. But there was nothing. So I went to the hardware store to talk to Gina's dad and her brother Emil to find out if they'd seen him. Emil often joined us at the pub, and sometimes he and Tony went without me if I was busy."

"What's Emil's last name?"

"Romano."

To Gina, Manziuk said, "And your father's name?"

"Joe Romano. Emil is my younger brother. Like Dom said, he and Tony and Emil were all friends."

"And neither Emil nor Joe had seen Tony that night?"

"That's what they told me," Dom said.

To Gina, Manziuk said, "What did you do next?"

"I somehow got through the day by pretending Tony had had to go into work, so as not to upset Felicia and Bruno. But Saturday night, when the kids were in bed, we gathered in Mama and Papa's rooms downstairs and talked about what we thought we should do. Some of us wanted to go back to the police, but the man I talked to had been so dismissive, it didn't seem worthwhile. And somebody said the police have a seventy-two-hour rule of some sort. So we decided to wait until Monday morning to go to them. And we just—

waited—and hoped he'd come home soon and everything would be okay." She looked down. "Only, of course, that didn't happen."

"For future information," Ryan said, "the seventy-two-hour rule doesn't exist. And I'm very sorry the officer you spoke to was so dismissive."

Felicia had been listening attentively. Now she spoke, "From what you've told us, it wouldn't have made any difference if the police *had* become involved earlier. Daddy was already dead, wasn't he?"

"That's very likely."

Dom stood up. "Well, you can make up for the police back then by catching the lowlife that did it."

THREE

A pudgy middle-aged man with long blondish-grey hair and a blue floral shirt was sweeping the floor of the barber shop when Ryan and Manziuk walked into Chiarelli's Barber Shop.

Ryan took the lead this time. "We're looking for Raphael Chiarelli."

The man frowned. "That's me. What can I do you for?"

Ryan showed him her ID. "We have a few questions concerning a former employee, Tony De Luca."

"Tony?"

"Yes."

"He's been gone a long, long time."

"Since October fifteenth, 1999."

"So, what's up?"

"Unfortunately, we've found Mr. De Luca's body."

Raphael's face turned white. "His body? Are you saying Tony's dead?"

"Yes."

"Recently?"

"In all likelihood, he died the night he disappeared."

Raphael dropped the broom and staggered over to collapse heavily onto one of the barber chairs. "Oh, my—I never wanted to believe that had happened." After a moment, he said, "What haven't you told me? Why are you here?"

"We're treating this as a homicide investigation."

Raphael shut his eyes.

Manziuk said, "Are you up to talking with us now?"

"I feel kind of faint. This—this is a shock. Just give me a minute."

"Can I get you something?" Ryan asked.

"Yeah, get me an energy drink from the fridge in my back office. You're welcome to anything you want from it, too."

As Ryan left the room, Raphael asked Manziuk to turn the sign on his front door to "Closed."

Fifteen minutes later, with Raphael's colour looking better, the three of them sat in a tight circle in chairs from the waiting area.

"Mr. Chiarelli," Ryan said, "what can you tell us about Tony De Luca?"

"He was a regular guy. Normal, you know? A good barber and a good person. I hated to lose him. And I never for one minute believed he'd leave his family."

"Did he have any enemies?"

Raphael shook his head. "Some of the customers might have preferred me to him, but then others preferred him to me. Nobody you'd call an enemy."

"Could there have been another woman?"

"If there was, he never said a word to me. Nor a man either, for that matter. He talked about his wife and kids a lot. Always had pictures if anybody asked. Or even if they didn't ask. He was so proud of them, especially the little girl. She was a firecracker. 'Precocious,' I think they call it. Always asking questions and coming up with stuff you'd never expect.

"He'd tell you he wasn't sure she was really his kid because she never got her brains from him. But it was a joke, you know? Anybody could see she was his kid. At a glance, she looks a lot like Gina, but if you look closer, you can see as much if not more of Tony in her features as well as in the way she walks and talks. As for Bruno, he's the spitting image of his dad."

"You still see them?" Ryan asked.

"Of course. Dom and Bruno come here to get their hair cut. And Papa De Luca—Mario—too."

"You say Tony left that night shortly after nine?"

"Just like usual. We stayed open until nine on Friday nights, and we each took one Saturday off in three. At nine, we locked the front door, swept up, and left."

"Who else was working here then?"

"A young guy. Cory. He was here for about two years, then moved out west."

"Was Cory here that Friday night?"

"No, there were only two of us at any time. Still normally that way. Except in quiet times, like now. My assistant is out for an early supper break. Cory and I were working that Saturday, so Tony was off that day, which is why at first the police apparently thought he was on a bender or something. But while he'd have a drink, it was nothing like what the police seemed to assume. I'm going by what Dom and Emil, Gina's brother, told me. Besides, Tony nearly always spent his Saturday off either with his kids or playing soccer."

Ryan leaned toward Raphael. "If I told you that Tony was killed that night—and that it could have happened right after he left here—does that change the way you look at the evening? Does anything come to mind?"

Raphael studied his feet. "No," he said. "It's like I thought then. Tony ran into somebody looking for a target to rob and tried to fight back, and the guy got violent." Raphael looked up. "How did he die? Can you tell me?"

"We think he was hit over the head with a blunt object or he fell against something hard."

Raphael shook his head. "I wish I could tell you something that would help you catch whoever was involved, but I've got nothing."

Manziuk spoke. "You and Tony got along well? You weren't planning on firing him or anything?"

Raphael's eyes grew large. "Firing him? Never! I told you, he was a good barber and a good guy. Ask anyone. We got along great. If anything, I might have made him a partner. And that's the truth. My guess, like I said, is that somebody saw him alone on the street and decided to rob him."

"But," Ryan said, "don't you think a stranger would have run away and left the body instead of going to the trouble of transporting it miles away and carrying it into the woods to bury it?"

Raphael stared from Ryan to Manziuk. "That's what happened?"

"It was found in the Don Valley."

"You think somebody Tony knew did this?"

Ryan nodded. "A co-worker, a friend, a family member…"

Raphael shut his eyes and swore.

Romano's Hardware was a few blocks west of the barber shop, on the north side of College Avenue. It was double the width of most of the smaller stores that lined the street, but not what anyone would call large. At least half of the window on the right was taken up with a sign that consisted of a large line-drawing of a bicycle and the words, "We specialize in bike repairs."

Manziuk and Ryan stepped onto the worn hardwood floor into a space crammed with old wooden shelves that sagged under the weight of assorted merchandise, from electric appliances to frying pans and bone china cups, from plastic storage containers to every kind of nail or screw, and from paint to a wide assortment of tools. Dotted along the end walls were larger items such as brooms, shovels, hampers, garbage cans, vacuums, and bicycles.

As they wandered through the aisles, Ryan shook her head. "Can you believe this place?" she whispered to Manziuk, who was ahead of her. "It's like a maze. How would you ever find anything?"

There were a couple of customers in the store, so Manziuk and Ryan waited for them to leave before approaching the counter.

"Joe Romano?" Manziuk said to the grey-haired man who had just closed the cash register and was watching them.

"Yes. What can I help you with?"

Manziuk introduced himself and Ryan, and asked Joe if he'd mind closing the store for a few minutes. "We have a few things we'd like to talk to you about."

Joe frowned. "Police?" In a louder voice, he said, "Emil, these people are with the police. They want us to close the store for a while."

His son, who had the same wavy dark brown hair as his sister, as well as the same mouth and grey eyes, came closer and stood with his legs apart and his arms crossed. "What is this about?"

Ryan stepped forward. "We'd like to talk to you in private about the death of Tony De Luca. We've already talked to his wife."

Joe said, "So it *is* him you found? Gina told us she'd had the police call on her a few days ago, but I thought it'd be a mistake."

Emil added, "You've already talked to Gina? She knows it's him?"

Manziuk said, "Yes, we talked to her and her family earlier today."

"Does Mario know?" Joe asked.

"Yes."

"How did he take it?"

"Do you have a sign you could put up for fifteen min-utes?" Ryan asked evenly. "So you don't have a customer come in while we're talking."

Joe motioned with his shoulder and Emil reluctantly walked to the front of the store and locked the door before putting up a small sign. Then he returned to the counter.

Manziuk explained about finding Tony's body and asked for help in their investigation.

"I'm sorry to hear he's dead," Emil said, "but I can't tell you anything."

Joe looked at his son and said, "Don't be silly, Emil. If there's something we can do to help, we'll be more than will-ing to do it."

"Pop, I never said I didn't want to help. But I can't tell them what I don't know. And I don't know any more about what happened to Tony now than I did back then."

A noise made them all turn toward the back of the store.

An attractive woman with long blond hair and what seemed to Ryan like an excess of makeup was strolling down the centre aisle toward them, a question on her face. She wore a sleeveless denim shirt, a pair of olive cargo pants, and sandals, but the outfit might have been an expensive evening gown from the way she walked.

Joe introduced her as Emil's wife, Lee, and explained to her why the police detectives were in the store.

Lee held her hand out to Manziuk and spoke in a husky voice, "Colour me astonished." She looked from her husband to her father-in-law and then back to Manziuk. "I've always believed Tony was alive and somewhere in the United States with a new name and another family. Now you tell me that he's been dead all this time—it's very shocking."

"Did you see him at any time on the day he disappeared?" Ryan asked.

"I didn't," Lee said.

"Did either of you?" Ryan looked from Joe to Emil.

Joe shook his head.

"No," Emil said. "When we closed the store that evening, I thought about wandering over to the pub where we used to hang out for a beer, but I had some things I wanted to finish up here, so I didn't go."

"What time did you leave the store?"

"I don't know. Close to midnight. Maybe a bit later. I was getting stuff done and I lost track of the time."

Ryan looked at Lee. "Do you remember when he came home that night?"

She shook her head. "I went to bed at about eleven-thirty, and I'm a sound sleeper."

"Were you at home all evening?"

"Yes."

"Were there children in the house? Or anyone else who could confirm that you were there?"

Lee smiled. "You mean give me an alibi? No. No children. And no one else. I watched television and had a couple of glasses of wine. I'd had a long day working a twelve-hour shift, from seven a.m. until seven p.m."

"Where did you work?"

"At a hospital. As a nurse."

Ryan looked at Joe. "And you, Mr. Romano? What did you do that evening?"

"I was here until nine. Then I walked down to meet some of my friends at a place some of us still go to. We broke up at about eleven. I guess a few of my friends might still be able to give me an alibi. Assuming they remember a night that long ago. I only remember it because of what happened afterwards."

Manziuk spoke. "Now that you all know what really happened, do you have any suggestions? Did Tony have a neighbour he disagreed with? Someone who didn't like a haircut? Did he play sports or have any hobbies? In other words, was there any way he could have made an enemy?"

Lee shrugged her shoulders.

Joe said, "Gina or Dom might know of someone. I don't."

"Have you talked to Raphael, his boss?" Emil asked.

"Yes."

"Well, I can't think of anybody," Emil said. "Tony and Dom both played soccer. Ask Dom."

"What about another woman?" Ryan asked.

The atmosphere became suddenly very tense.

Lee said, "Not that I'm aware of. But I guess I might not have known."

"If there'd been even a suggestion of another woman," Emil said, "I'd have knocked his head off."

"Are you nearly done with these stupid questions?" Joe asked, his eyes flashing anger. "This is getting you nowhere. None of us can think of any reason why someone would want to kill Tony. You should be looking for some crazy with a few screws loose instead of bothering his family."

Ryan had arranged for Dom to meet them at 5:30 in the pub that currently occupied the space where he and Tony were supposed to meet the night Tony disappeared.

"It looked nothing like this back then," Dom said as Manziuk and Ryan joined him in front of a fireplace at a small triangular table with three leather easy chairs. On the walls were paintings by local artists, and the menu included lattes, speciality teas, espressos, cocktails, select wines and beer, and organic snacks.

A waitress appeared and the men ordered coffees while Ryan picked a white chai tea.

Dom leaned forward with his elbows on the table. "You said on the phone that you want me to go over what I remember from that day. I don't know that I can tell you anything more than I already said back at the house. Trust me, I've gone over it a thousand times over the years, and I always come up blank."

"Let's start with this place," Manziuk said. "What was it like then?"

"It was a regular pub for working class people. Mostly men, but some women. They served beer and wine as well as harder drinks, but mostly beer. Quite a few kinds. And some food. But nothing healthy, you know? Pizza, chicken wings, garlic bread, that sort of thing. And TV screens, of course, with hockey games. Soccer when it was available. Tony and I met here for a beer at least one night a week, sometimes two or three."

"So it was normal for you to meet on Friday just after nine o'clock?"

"Yeah. But not every Friday. Just on nights he worked late. When he didn't work, either he and Gina did something with the kids or they went on a date. Sometimes she came here with him, too."

"His parents babysat?"

"That's right. They were already in the house, so it wasn't a big deal. They had an intercom so they could hear the kids if they woke up. Papa De Luca has always been good at rigging up electronic gadgets."

"So that particular Friday, you were here by nine, and you waited how long?"

"I got here about ten after nine. And it isn't as if I sat here staring at my watch. I was talking to people and watching the game on TV. Like I said back at the house, it didn't even register on me until nearly ten that Tony hadn't shown up. I just figured something had come up. Or he'd told me he wasn't coming and I'd forgotten. It isn't as if we planned this out like an appointment or something. It was just, if we were both there, we'd have a beer together."

"On Saturday," Ryan said, "when you found out he hadn't gone home, what did you think?"

"I thought the cops were nuts! No way he'd just take off. But I thought you had to wait seventy-two hours before the police would look for him. By Monday morning, we were all frantic. We knew it was bad. And at that point, the cops finally believed us. Sort of. But they assumed he'd either gone off to kill himself or he'd gone off with another woman. Nothing we could say changed their minds." He shrugged. "I guess you can't blame them. There was no body and no reason to think that anything had happened to him. Still, I wish we'd known the truth. It wouldn't have helped Tony, but it could have saved years of wondering and trying to make sense of it."

After Dom left, Manziuk and Ryan ordered mango salads with chicken breasts and went over what they'd learned, which was pretty well nothing.

Manziuk phoned Benson and told him to go ahead and release the identity of the body and add a note requesting anyone who might have information to contact the police or Crimestoppers. He also asked if Evan had found the dog yet.

"No, but I'm meeting him in the parking lot tonight at eight and walking to the spot where Evan has a trap set up. That way, I can get more details about how he came to find the dog and the skull and get the story ready for publication."

Manziuk smiled. "I hope you find the dog soon."

After hanging up, he repeated what Benson had said to Ryan, who laughed and said, "I hope the results are worth the effort."

Manziuk waited while the waitress poured him a fresh cup of coffee before leaning back and saying, "So, one question we should probably ask is, 'Who gains—in this case, I guess it's who *gained*—from Tony's death?'"

"That's easy," Ryan said. "Dom Marino got a wife and family out of it."

"Right. But for all we know, perhaps Gina benefited the most. Maybe her marriage wasn't as rosy as everyone says. Maybe Tony wasn't a great husband and father. So she got a new husband."

Ryan slammed her hand on the table. "So far, everybody's had only good to say about Tony. What if they're all lying?"

"All?"

"You know, to protect his name or something. Maybe he was actually a jerk but they don't want to say anything because of his father or—or his kids! What if they don't want his kids to know what their father was really like?"

Manziuk frowned.

"What if they didn't want to draw attention to it, so they took care of it themselves?" Ryan said.

"Are you suggesting they were all in it together?"

"It's possible. We've been accepting what they said as if it were true, but what if they're all lying?"

"Well, that might be possible, but it's the kind of thing that would work in an Agatha Christie novel, not so much in real life."

Ryan bit her lower lip. "You always say we need to keep our minds open to all possibilities."

"True, but we have to start with the most likely scenario and go from there."

"And what's the most likely scenario?"

"That it was a robbery." Manziuk finished his coffee.

"But you said yourself that a common thief wouldn't have moved the body."

"The next likely scenario is that it was someone he knew."

"Right."

"*Some*one. Not everyone."

"Okay, I'll grant you that. For now." She took a final sip of her tea. "You've also told me that most people keep something back. Something that's embarrassing, or that they think is irrelevant, or that they've forgotten."

"Definitely. It's also not unusual for people to see past events through rose-coloured glasses when it involves someone close to them. So you're right. Tony might not have been as perfect as everyone has suggested."

"How do we get them to tell us the truth?"

Manziuk leaned back and put his hands on his upper thighs. "Well, since it happened so long ago, let's start with the first thing we talked about—those who benefited from his death."

"Okay. Where do we start?"

"With the people we talked to today."

"Okay." She thought for a moment. "I can't see any way Raphael benefited—assuming he was telling the truth about thinking of making Tony a partner. Otherwise, he was the boss—he could have just fired him. Tony's wife and parents. Not really. His father-in-law, brother-in-law, and sister-in-law?"

She shrugged. "I can't see that they've benefited. Which brings us back to Dom. He's the most obvious one."

"Agreed." Manziuk stretched. "And tomorrow, that's where we'll start. But now, we may as well call it a day. This case has been waiting nearly seventeen years. It can wait another few hours."

"Maybe we'll have some brilliant insights overnight."

"I'm not holding my breath," Manziuk said. "If this *was* a random killing, we'll hit a dead end soon. And if it wasn't, we still may hit a dead end."

"But we have to try, right?"

"All right. Let's sleep on it and see what comes up tomorrow."

They drove back to headquarters and headed to their respective homes: Manziuk to his wife, Ryan to the crowded row house that was bursting at the seams with five women sharing it.

As Jacquie Ryan stepped inside the house, she heard voices coming from the front room. She took off her shoes and set down her purse before walking down the hallway and turning left. Her mother, grandmother, aunt, and cousin were sitting on the chesterfield and chairs, deep in discussion.

Noelle Ryan, Jacquie's mother, said, "Oh, Jacquie's here. Good. We need your opinion."

"On what?"

"On whether or not we need to update the kitchen."

"The kitchen?" Jacquie frowned. Her grandmother did most of the cooking, and Jacquie had never heard her complain. "What's wrong with it?"

Grams said, "Nothing."

Jacquie's mother said, "Everything."

Aunt Vida said, "It needs new appliances, new flooring, and new cupboards. Likely the plumbing and wiring need to be redone, too."

Vida's daughter, Precious, said, "It's old as the hills. It's embarrassing when my friends see it."

"It doesn't need a single thing," Grams said.

The other three women groaned or shook their heads.

"Three questions," Jacquie said. "Is anything actually not working? Not up to building code? Dangerous to use? Second, how much money are we talking about? And third, where would the money come from?"

"Everything is fine," her grandmother said, "and I should know. I do most of the cooking. Besides, this is *my* house." She stood up, her lower lip quivering. "You all moved in with me when you needed a place to stay, and I was glad to have you. But now you want to tell me what I have to do with my house. Well, if you don't like it here, you know what you can do." She walked to the bottom of the stairs. "I'm going to my room now. I'm tired."

After Grams left, her daughters and granddaughters didn't say a word for several minutes. Finally, Jacquie said, "Well, I hope you're all happy."

"It's so unfair!" Precious said. "Nobody ever cares how I feel." She jumped up and ran up the stairs to her room, and slammed her door.

Jacquie looked at her mother and her aunt, rolled her eyes, and ran up the stairs to her own room. She was tired and her brain was toast. They'd have to work this one out without her.

Breakfast on Friday morning had gone so well that Felicia Marino and Evan McEwan had arranged to meet at six-thirty Saturday morning in the parking lot nearest to the spot where Evan had set up the live trap.

When Felicia drove up, Evan was standing on the grass near his car, stretching. She watched him for a second, wondering if this was as good an idea as it had seemed yesterday. Maybe she should have brought a friend along. After all, what did she know about Evan other than that he had brought her dad's body to the attention of the police? Didn't they say the person who found a body was often involved?

Of course, Evan would have only been seven when her dad died. So that let him out. Unless maybe he was the son of the actual killer and his father had confessed on his death bed, and Evan had released the dog and then used it as an excuse to "find" the body.

Oh, man! She was letting her imagination go bonkers! Evan was who he said he was. A nice guy who wanted to be a veterinarian. Single. And perfectly safe. Besides, she had her mobile phone along and could call 911 if she had a problem. Plus her mother knew where she was. Knew, but wasn't at all happy about it. They hadn't told Dom. He wouldn't have been happy at all. But Felicia had recently turned twenty-three—more than old enough to make her own decisions.

Evan walked over to the car and Felicia quickly got out.

"Good morning," he said. "Having second thoughts?"

"Kind of."

"You don't have to come if you don't want to."

"I want to. It's all just so—surreal—you know?"

He nodded.

They began jogging along the path, Evan in the lead.

Half an hour later, they'd checked the trap, which held a pacing raccoon. Making sure Felicia stayed well back, Evan released the raccoon, which glared at him before waddling off. Evan then refilled the water and kibble dishes before resetting the trap.

While he was doing this, Felicia wandered over to the crime scene tape and stood staring at the place where her father's bones had been found.

Evan came up behind her.

"I wish I could picture him more clearly," she said. "I remember how I felt around him more than I do him, if that makes sense."

"I think so."

"When he was around, I felt warm, safe, happy…"

"And after he was gone?"

"Confused. They told me that he didn't want to go away, but that he had to. I kept asking why, but no one would tell me. Of course, the truth was they had no idea what to tell me because they didn't know any more than I did. But all I knew was that my daddy was gone and everyone cried all the time. Everyone except Dom."

"Dom?"

"My step-dad. He was my dad's best friend. Dom is really the one who got all of us through those days. He brought food from restaurants so Mom and Mama De Luca didn't have to cook, and he helped me with my schoolwork, and he took Bruno and me to the park so Mom could have some time to herself, and he did other things, too. Things Daddy would have done if he'd been there."

She turned to look at Evan. "Honestly, when I think back, I'm not sure we'd have survived without Dom. He wasn't my daddy, but he took his place. And, gradually, my real dad became a vague memory. My brother Bruno doesn't even remember him. Of course, he was only three. Later, when Dom and Mom got married, it was the natural thing to do."

Evan leaned against a tree. "Do you have any memories from the days before your dad disappeared that might help the police?"

"Like what?"

"Well, do you remember your dad ever fighting with anyone? Or arguing?"

She shook her head. "He wasn't like that. I remember him laughing a lot. And teasing Mom. Making her giggle. And playing games with me. He'd come to tea parties with my dolls and drink the pretend tea and eat the pretend pastries and tell jokes."

"Do you remember anything from the day when they found out he was missing? It must have been unusual."

Felicia crossed her arms. "I remember waking up that Saturday morning and going to the kitchen and finding Mama De Luca sitting at the table crying," she said softly. "My mother and Papa Luca were there, too. Dom was telling them not to worry. I remember him saying, 'Tony can look after himself.'" Felicia reached into her pocket for a tissue and wiped her eyes.

"You're doing great," Evan said. "What else do you remember?"

She gave him a wry smile. "I was standing in the doorway, and when I heard Dom say that, I asked what they were talking about. Mom said not to worry, and to go and play with Bruno. But I asked if we were still going to Centre Island that day, and Mom said, 'Your Daddy didn't come home last night, but he'll be home soon.' And I said, 'Yes, he did, I saw him.'" Felicia felt a chill go through her. "I honestly remember saying that."

"What happened next?"

She thought for a moment, then said, "Mom told me I couldn't have seen him. I started to argue, but Papa De Luca told me to be a good girl and go play with Bruno, so I did."

Evan was staring at her. "What do you think you meant when you said you saw him?"

"I—I don't know. I hadn't remembered that until now. But I can see it clearly. They were sitting around the kitchen table, and I was standing in the doorway, and they were all staring at me, just like you are now."

"Sorry." He smiled. "I got so caught up in what you were saying that I could see it myself. So, do you think you really did see your dad?"

"I remember insisting that I had. But Mom told me I was wrong."

"Had you been out of your bedroom the night before?"

She shook her head. "I don't think so."

"What time did you go to bed?"

"Around eight-thirty, I think."

"And what did you do then? Go right to sleep?"

"No. I kept some books on my nightstand, and Mom let me read for a while."

"I thought you said you were six."

"I was. But I started reading when I was around four and a half. I could read most of my picture books by the time I was six."

"I think I should start feeling intimidated about now."

"And here I was thinking it was really hard to get into vet school. I've heard it's even harder than medical school."

Evan grinned. "Well, I like to think I have a few brains."

"Do smart women scare you?"

"Not at all. Just the opposite, in fact."

"Really?"

"Yes, really. My parents are both very smart people, and equal partners in every way. I want the same thing. I think it makes for an exciting, happy family."

"Huh."

"Is that so strange?"

"Not strange. Just kind of unusual. I broke up with someone a few months ago because he hated the fact that I'm in a PhD program."

"What's your goal?"

"Helping families who lose a parent. It's kind of an obsession of mine."

"You have a Masters?"

"Got it this spring."

"Sounds intriguing."

"I guess maybe you can understand it. Only your thing is helping animals."

"Exactly."

"So, getting back to that Friday night. You went to bed, but not to sleep?"

"Yes. I read for a while and then turned the light off. But I often continued to read under the covers. I had a small flashlight." She grinned. "I've always loved books."

Evan smiled back. "Me, too."

"My door was always shut, and there were some boards in the hallway that creaked, so I had time to pretend I was asleep whenever anybody looked in. But after I went to bed, I normally didn't go out of my room except once in a while to go to the bathroom."

"With the creaky boards, do you think you'd have heard your father if he'd come home shortly after nine and walked down the hallway?"

"Yes. But I didn't say I'd *heard* him. I said I *saw* him."

Evan thought for a moment. "Could your dad have come into your room that night?"

She thought for a moment, then shook her head. "No."

"Was there any other way you could have seen him?"

Felicia looked at her feet. "I'm picturing my room and the bed and me as a little kid, and—" She looked up. "Of course! The window. My bed used to be beside the window, which looks out on our front yard. When I was younger, I'd get on my knees on the bed so I could lean my elbows on the windowsill and look out. Our house is across from a park, so it's often busy. There's always someone walking down the sidewalk, or a car driving down the street. Plus, there's a streetlight in front of the house next door, which helped me see." She stared at Evan and spoke in small voice. "I remember. I looked out my window and saw him. I was certain it was him."

"Could you have made a mistake? I mean, could it have been somebody else?"

"I guess. But I really thought it was him." She felt cold again. "Evan," she whispered, "what if I *did* see him that night?"

Evan frowned. "Do you think that your mother and your other relatives could have—well, known what happened to him, but for some reason lied about it? I know that sounds ridiculous, but—"

"It *is* ridiculous," Felicia said. "You didn't live with a mother who cried as if her heart would break for years. So many times, I came into the sitting room and found Mom sitting in the rocking chair holding my dad's picture, with tears streaming down her cheeks. And sometimes I heard her whisper, 'Oh, Tony, where are you? Why did you leave us? Please, please, come home.' And sometimes I heard her praying, 'God, if Tony can't come home, please find a way to let me know.' My mother had nothing to do with my father's death. You can take that to the bank. And my grandparents, too. He was their only son. Ours was a house of sadness for most of Bruno's and my childhood."

"So, how could it be possible that *you* saw him but your mother didn't?"

Felicia turned to look toward the trees, and thought hard, willing herself to remember. "The image I have is of Daddy facing our house while he was talking to someone who had his back to me. The two of them were on the sidewalk that went by the front of our house. And then I *think* they walked across the street toward the park."

She turned back to Evan. "I need to tell the police." She shivered. "I don't know if they'll believe me, though."

"They seem to be pretty easy to talk to. The ones I've met, anyway."

"I'll send a text to Constable Ryan. But let's get out of here first. This place is too depressing."

Four

Paul Manziuk was about to have breakfast when Ryan called him. After a short conversation, he turned to his wife. "Can you make me a sandwich to go?"

Loretta Manziuk frowned. "What is it?"

"The daughter of the man whose body was found thinks she remembers something from the night he went missing. Which was nearly seventeen years ago. When she was six. It's doubtful that what she has to tell us will be useful, but Ryan told her we'd meet with her right away."

Their son, Michael, a senior in high school, walked into the room. "Dad, what do you think about—"

"I'm really sorry, Mike. We'll have to talk later. Or maybe you could send me an email." Paul hurried from the room to get his shoes and grab his suit jacket.

This was the only part of his job that he hated: need for immediacy, which often meant not being there for his family. Yet, at the same time, the urgency was a big part of what he loved about his job.

When he returned to the kitchen, Loretta handed him a plastic-wrapped sandwich made from two pieces of toast and slices of ham and tomato.

"Is Mike okay?"

"It was nothing urgent. Don't worry. Mike understands."

Manziuk gave his wife a quick kiss on the cheek before heading out to his car. Ryan had asked Felicia to meet them at police headquarters.

When Manziuk and Ryan followed Felicia into the kitchen as the Marinos were finishing their breakfast, Gina and Dom looked up in shock. Their two younger sons were also at the table, and Gina quickly sent them upstairs to get dressed and clean their rooms.

Dom stood up. "What is this?" he asked. "Why are you bothering my daughter?"

"*Your* daughter?" Manziuk asked quietly.

Dom crossed his arms. "Yes, *mine*. I'm her father and she's my daughter. And don't pretend my saying that is a bad thing. It isn't."

Felicia walked toward Dom and put her arm around him. "Dad, it's okay. They're only doing their job. I've remembered something. I don't know if it's significant or not."

Dom narrowed his eyes as he looked down at her. "What are you talking about?"

"That Saturday morning when you were here talking, I remember saying that I'd seen my daddy the night before."

"You couldn't have. Your mother said he wasn't here."

"That's not exactly true, Mr. Marino," Ryan said. "Gina told us that if he *was* here he'd left no trace."

"But…"

"Dad, just listen," Felicia said. "Please."

Dom sighed. "Okay. What is it?"

"When I wasn't sleepy at night, I sometimes looked out my window. The image I have in my mind from that night is of seeing Daddy out front talking to someone."

"Who?" Dom asked.

"I don't know. They were on the sidewalk out in front of the house. Daddy was facing our house, but the person he was talking to—I *think* it was a man, but it might have been a woman—had his back toward me."

Gina had been listening with a sceptical look on her face. Now she stepped forward, shaking her head. "You're imaging it, Felicia. They're been filling your head with possibilities and now you think you remember something, but you don't."

"Mom, I have a master's degree in psychology, remember? I know all about false memories. But I clearly remember telling you all that I'd seen Daddy the night before. Don't you remember?"

"No, I don't."

"I do," Dom said slowly. "Now that you remind me, I remember you saying that. But you were what? Six? We thought you were saying it to get attention because we'd been ignoring you."

Gina said, "Maybe you're confusing it with something you saw another time."

Felicia shook her head. "All I know is that when I said it that morning, I believed it. And I have this memory—like a dark black and white image—of seeing them outside my window in the streetlight, and knowing it was Daddy."

Gina looked at Manziuk. "Inspector, what does this mean? If Felicia is right, and she did see him that night, will it help you find out what happened?"

"We're going to do our best."

"But if she really did see Tony, who could he have been talking to?"

Felicia looked from Manziuk to Ryan. "You think he was killed by someone he knew, don't you? That it wasn't just a robbery gone wrong?"

"We're leaning in that direction," Manziuk said.

"Because of where he was found?"

"Yes."

"No!" Gina began to sob. "No one who knew him would have wanted to kill Tony! I don't believe it!"

As Felicia bent to comfort her, Dom motioned to Manziuk and Ryan, and the three of them quietly left the house.

As he led the way down the front steps, Dom said, "What about the possibility it was some total stranger who was just looking for a thrill? That happens, doesn't it? Didn't that guy get killed a few years ago by a total stranger who pretended he wanted to test drive a truck before buying it? And the guy tried to burn the body or something?"

"Yes," Manziuk said. "Things like that are rare, but not impossible."

Dom kicked a pebble onto the grass. "This sucks." He looked up. "Don't get me wrong. I'm glad we know what happened to Tony, but trying to dig up the past means rehashing everything. It's going to hurt."

"I'm afraid so," Manziuk said. "But I find that most people want to know the truth."

"Yeah. And I know for a fact that Felicia won't let it go. Joe, too, likely." Dom took a deep breath and let it out. "So what's next? Do you believe Felicia saw Tony that night?"

"You know her better than we do," Ryan said. "What do you think?"

Dom threw the question back to her. "How much do *you* remember from when you were six?"

"Actually, quite a bit. We came to Canada when I was five. I remember living in Jamaica, and I remember the plane ride here, and what it was like coming to a new house, and starting school…. I remember a lot. Especially things that were meaningful. I think she'd have memories from the day her father disappeared. Do you not remember being six?"

"Maybe a few things," he said. "But, more important, I remember her saying that she'd seen him. And all of us telling her it was impossible." There was a long pause. "So, what's next?"

Manziuk looked at the park across the street. "If we assume her memory is real, then I guess we have to assume that she saw them walk across the street to the park."

"Well, since her memory is all we have to go on as yet," Ryan said, "let's check it out."

"It'll have changed in seventeen years," Manziuk said.

"You don't really think he might have been killed here?" Dom asked.

Manziuk said, "It's possible."

Dom shut his eyes as if in pain, then opened them and nodded. "Okay. If that's the way it is, we can't change it." He moved toward the street. "Gina's lived across from this park for more than twenty years. Papa De Luca even longer. And I've been going to it for most of my life."

Manziuk and Ryan followed.

When they returned to police headquarters, Ryan and Manziuk met with Ford to find out what the Ident Team had learned.

"Not much," Ford said. "We've done background checks, and the De Lucas, Dom Marino, and the Romanos are all clear. Nobody has a police record. Well, Lee Romano has had a few speeding tickets, but that's it."

"Tell us everything you've learned, even if it seems innocuous," Manziuk said. "Something might stick out."

"Okay, I'll start with Tony's parents. Mario De Luca was a well-respected carpenter until he retired a few years ago. He made hand-crafted one-of-a-kind furniture. Still does some work, but only for former clients. His wife Silvana was primarily a homemaker but also took care of the paperwork for his business. She was also a devout Catholic. She had at least five pregnancies, but only the one son, Tony, survived.

"Tony was a good athlete who played football and soccer in high school. He was also an avid soccer fan. After high school, he trained as a barber, got a job, and got married. He and Gina Romano had been a twosome since they were in grade ten but knew each other most of their lives. Her family had a house on the next street over from the De Lucas, about four blocks south. Her dad still lives there.

"Gina's father, Joe Romano, has owned his hardware store for nearly thirty years. His wife, Gina's mother, died when Gina was twenty from breast cancer. There's one son, Emilio—they call him Emil, who is a partner in the hardware store. Emil's wife Lee is a registered nurse. No kids.

"Dom Marino is the youngest of six kids. His father was a real estate agent who did really well for himself and retired ten years ago. He and his wife have a condo in Florida and a cottage in the Muskokas, and they divide the year between the two places.

"Dom and Tony were friends from elementary school. Dom started his own real estate agency and has done reasonably well. Seems to be well liked. He married Gina more than six years after Tony's death, and they had two more kids—sons.

"The other names you gave me were the barbers Raphael Chiarelli and Cory Perkins. Raphael had a bit of a rocky adolescence—mostly skipping school and possible drug use, with a couple of ventures into dealing. But since his marriage, he's kept his nose clean.

"Cory Perkins was working for Raphael at the same time as Tony, and left a few months after Tony disappeared, but he'd been planning to move to Alberta where his fiancée lived. He's got a barber shop in Red Deer along with a wife and four kids. Seems like a regular guy. Nothing to indicate he was running away from a murder."

Manziuk said, "Good work."

Ford shrugged. "Doesn't really get us anywhere, does it?"

Manziuk said, "We may end up deciding Tony didn't know his killer, but I'm still bothered by the idea that someone he didn't know would go to all the work of hiding his body where it was. Think about it. The body wasn't just dumped somewhere or buried in a place that was easy to access. It was hidden so well it wasn't found for nearly seventeen years! That's really the only reason I have for assuming it wasn't a random killing."

Ryan said, "Could a friend of his have met him outside the barber shop, driven him home, killed him in the park across the street, and then put his body in the car and taken it to the woods to bury it?"

Ford stared at her. "Huh? What do you two know that I don't?"

With Ryan adding details, Manziuk filled Ford in on Felicia's memory fragment and their visit to the park.

"So," Manziuk said, "if we assume his killer knew him, I'm leaning toward the idea that it may have happened in the heat of the moment rather than being premeditated. There are trees, a brick building, picnic tables, and a bunch of cement blocks which I assume are used as benches. I'm willing to bet it was much the same seventeen years ago. It isn't hard for me to believe that Tony and whoever he was talking to had a fight, and Tony died when he fell against something hard. And then the killer panicked and tried to hide the body."

Ford frowned. "Dr. Wong said there were two separate skull fractures. Wouldn't the first one have put him out of commission?"

Manziuk shook his head. "Not necessarily. People do crazy things, like playing football or hockey with a broken leg. Have you seen all the new stuff on concussions? People have ignored them for years. Laughed about 'getting your bell rung' or 'seeing stars.' We checked with Dr. Weaver. Tony could have fallen, hit his head, shaken it off, and jumped up—all without realizing he had the fracture—and, I assume—the concussion. But when he was hit the second time, he didn't get up."

"Makes sense," Ford said. "If it was premeditated, he'd have likely been hit over the head from behind with the proverbial blunt instrument, and then hit a second time after he was down. Given what we know about him, an argument, and then an accidental death with the other person panicking, seems more logical."

"If that's the case, it would have been manslaughter," Ryan said.

"Maybe. It's hard to say." Ford looked from one to the other. "Okay, assuming we have a working theory, how about I see if my team can find any kind of connection between someone on our list and the burial site?"

Manziuk agreed, and Ford left.

"Assuming Felicia's memory is accurate," Ryan said, "the person Tony was talking to could have been his father, his father-in-law, Dom, Raphael, or Emil. Or even Gina or Lee, I guess. But it also could have been somebody else—a customer, someone he played football or soccer with, a neighbour, someone he knew from a bar… So where do we start?"

"I think we have to start with the people in his immediate circle," Manziuk said. "Once we eliminate them, we can go beyond." He leaned forward. "However, we have to remember that the people we're going to talk to aren't necessarily guilty of anything. So while we have to ask hard questions, we can't treat them as if they're hardened criminals."

"Right," Ryan said. "But so far, we've been treating them with kid gloves. It's time we start asking hard questions."

"Judiciously."

"Another angle to look at is who would have been strong enough to carry his body all that distance into the woods to bury it."

"Dom, Emil, maybe Raphael? I'm not sure about Joe or Mario. They'd have been younger then, of course. Maybe around my current age. But I'd have a very hard time carrying a body down the path into those woods."

"Maybe he had help."

"I suppose. Or maybe we're missing something."

Ryan grinned. "That's entirely possible."

"So who do you think we should talk to first?"

"I'd say Gina Marino is the obvious person."

Manziuk thought for a moment, then nodded. "I agree."

"She's going to be thrilled to see us again. Not!"

Gina Marino stared at Ryan. "You were already here this morning."

"We have more questions about the night your husband died. Are you able to talk to us now?"

"I guess so. My younger boys are at a friend's house. But I don't know what more I can tell you about that night. All I can tell you is that I put my children to bed, watched TV, and then went to bed. No one saw me."

"I'm sorry," Ryan said, "but in a murder investigation we have to go over things more than once because people often remember more details later on. If you want to us to find out the truth about what happened, you'll need to let us ask our questions."

Gina put one hand up to her face and then stood aside. "Please, come in and sit down." She waited until Ryan and Manziuk had found seats in the sitting room, then perched on the edge of a straight chair and crossed her arms. "As I said before, that night I made supper and I played a few games with the kids—"

"What games?" Ryan asked.

"What games? I— Let me think." Gina looked at the far wall. "Felicia was six and Bruno was three. I can't say for sure we played them that night, but I can tell you roughly what we might have done. We often played Hide and Seek. And Blue's Clues. Candy Land. And we built towers with blocks." Gina leaned forward and clasped her hands around her knees. "We had some tapes of children's songs and I'd play them and we'd dance to them and act silly. And then I'd read some books to quieten them down.

"Because he was younger, I'd put Bruno to bed first, and then Felicia and I would do some girlie things, like setting out her clothes for the next day. Oh, now that I think of it, she had a jewellery kit we got for her that summer, and on the weekends, after Bruno was in bed, I'd help her make things. And I'd get her to read to me because we were working on her reading." She looked at Manziuk as if challenging him to argue. "She learned to read before she went to school."

Her gaze returned to the far wall, and she settled back in the chair. "Anyway, I put Felicia to bed a little before nine, and then I watched television for an hour. I don't remember which show it was. I went to bed just after the show ended at ten."

Ryan looked up from her laptop. "Is it possible that your husband came home after you were asleep, but you didn't hear him?"

Gina looked over at her. "Yes, it's possible, but I didn't go to sleep until after eleven. I read until then. If he came in after that, I might not have heard him." She changed her position on the chair, leaning forward again. "But if Tony *did* come home, he didn't leave any signs. His side of the bed wasn't rumpled. He didn't use his toothbrush or razor or any dishes or glasses. And there was nothing missing. The police made me check. None of his clothes were gone. And none of his toiletries or anything that meant something to him— his soccer and football trophies, the photo of his parents he kept on his nightstand, the photo of me and the kids that he loved, the extra money that he kept in his closet for emergencies.… Not a single thing was missing."

"You said earlier that at the time, you thought he must be dead."

"Yes. Dead or imprisoned."

"Who did you suspect of harming him?"

"Who? I don't know who. But if somebody tried to rob him, I think he might have fought back. That's what I've always believed happened. And this doesn't change it." She shook her head. "I don't think we'll ever know who did it. Not now."

"Did Tony ever argue with your brother or Dom?"

Gina frowned. "No."

"They never disagreed?"

"Of course, they disagreed. About soccer and hockey games and things like that. But they never argued in an angry way. They would bet on games sometimes—just small amounts of money—and then they'd argue for hours about why the others were wrong, but afterwards they'd discuss what happened and joke about it, the way men do."

"So you don't recall a time when they were really angry with one another?"

She shook her head. "No. Never."

Manziuk asked, "When did you get rid of your husband's clothing and possessions?"

Gina gave him a questioning look. "I left them where they were for a long time. Years. After Dom and my lawyer persuaded me to file in court that Tony be declared dead, I realized I needed to go through his things. Papa De Luca and I did it. Mama couldn't."

"What did you do?"

"We sorted his clothes, and we steeled ourselves to give things away. We gave a few to Dom and Emil, and Papa kept a few, but most of them went to a charity. All but a few we couldn't part with. His football and soccer jerseys. The suit he wore when we were married. Things like that."

"What about non-clothing items?"

"His toiletries we had to throw out. We gave away his sports equipment and his magazines and most of his music. Some of his things—like that drawing on the wall above the loveseat—are still around the house, and the others we packed up and put into a couple of boxes. I still have them."

Ryan stood and looked at the picture on the wall. It was a framed ink drawing of a younger Mario De Luca with his arm around a laughing Gina, who looked much like Felicia did now. "Who drew this?"

"Tony did. He liked to relax by doodling, and sometimes he drew people."

"It's very good," Manziuk said.

"Yes, we thought he ought to draw more, but he only did it now and then. There's another of the two of us and the kids in my bedroom if you want to see it."

"Could we see the other things, too?" Ryan asked. "The ones in the boxes?"

"I guess so."

Manziuk asked, "Did he keep a diary or a notebook of any sort?"

"Just an appointment book. There wasn't much in it."

"We'd like to see everything."

Gina stood. "All right. They're in the storage room in the basement. I'll show you. But first I need to tell Papa De Luca what we're doing. I don't want him to be upset."

"Why don't we go and talk to him first?" Manziuk said.

Gina sat back down. "Please. You know the way."

Mario De Luca didn't say anything when Manziuk told him they wanted to look through what remained of his son's belongings. He just sighed and led them to a door outside of his apartment, near the stairs. The door opened into a small, narrow room lined on both sides by shelves which were filled with plastic bins and boxes. Mario showed them two bins and said they could open them in his sitting room, but he wouldn't watch.

Manziuk and Ryan each carried a bin.

Inside both were mementos from Tony's childhood and youth: football and soccer trophies, several jerseys, a team jacket, two pairs of cleats, a Blue Jays baseball cap, a winter cap with ear flaps, a brown leather jacket. At the bottom of one box were a couple of flat rectangular boxes.

The first box held important papers—his birth certificate, passport, a certificate from a hairdressing school, numerous individual and group photos of soccer and football teams, and so forth.

The other box had pen and ink pictures he must have drawn; they all had his signature in the lower right corner. Like the ones they'd seen upstairs, these were very good. Not amazing, maybe, but you knew who the people were, and you caught a sense of their essence. Five of them in particular stood out: Gina as a radiant bride, Felicia as a little girl with a delightful secret, Bruno as a laughing baby, Mario with a twinkle in his eye, and his arm around the shoulders of a smiling woman they assumed was his wife, Tony's mother. Ryan got the sense that she was looking at the artist with pride.

Ryan looked at Manziuk through tears. "All this tells me is that he was a very nice, young man. There's nothing to indicate why anyone would kill him."

Manziuk nodded. "I really can't believe his wife or his father would have had anything to do with his death."

"Agreed."

"Let's move on to Dom."

They returned the items to the bins and put the bins back in the storage room.

Mario De Luca was seated at his kitchen table when they went back to his apartment.

"Mr. De Luca," Manziuk said, "do you have any reason at all to think that Dom Marino could have killed your son? Either intentionally or by accident?"

"Dom? You want to know if I think *Dom* killed Tony? Never. You need to get new jobs as garbage collectors."

The old man got to his feet. He was scowling, and his eyes flashed with anger. "What gives you the right to come into my house and ask me a question like this, or upset Gina and the kids? This nonsense isn't going to help you find out how Tony died, and it's not going to bring back my son. Now, go!"

"We're sorry to upset you," Manziuk said, "but please understand that we have to ask these questions. Whoever killed Tony might have killed other people. Might still be dangerous. We have to follow every possibility, and we have to begin by talking to those who knew Tony best, even if it means asking troublesome questions."

Mario looked down at the floor.

After a few minutes, he nodded. "I understand." He sank back onto his chair, his head on his hands.

Ryan sat on a chair beside him and placed her hand gently on his back. "Other than Dom, who else was close to your son?"

Mario's voice was gruff. "Emil, Gina's brother. He and Lee were around a lot in those days. They still are. Maybe not as much as when they were younger, but a lot. Joe, Gina's dad. We were—we still are—a tight-knit family."

"Anyone else?"

"Raphael, his boss. Tony thought a lot of him. And there were lots of others, but they were casual friends. Teammates, people from the pub, his customers. None of them would have had any reason to hurt Tony."

❦

"Well, that told us," Ryan said as she closed the door to the basement apartment and followed Manziuk down the sidewalk to their car.

"I can't really blame him," Manziuk said. "It's not enough that he knows his son is dead, but we're stirring up all the old memories."

"People always say they want closure."

"And they do. But this is the part of the job I dislike the most. Yes, we want to find the truth, but in order to do that, we have to assume that people close to the victim could be guilty. To an innocent person, who just wants to grieve the loss of a loved one, our questions must seem like torture."

"Getting at the truth is worth it in the end," Ryan said.

"I hope so."

"Who's next?"

"Let's take the rest of the family, one by one. Then we'll talk to his boss again."

FIVE

om Marino was seated at his desk with a jumble of papers in front of him. He looked up when his secretary showed Manziuk and Ryan into his office. When they told him why they were there, he stood up. "You want to check my alibi? I've already told you everything. You don't believe me?"

"If you could just tell us exactly, moment by moment, what you remember," Ryan said.

"I already told you. I was at the bar."

"What time did you leave?"

"I told you. Around eleven. Maybe a little before. I didn't check. It's not like anybody was waiting up for me."

"Did you walk or drive?"

"I had my car."

"Where was it?"

"On the street. At a meter."

"What kind of car?" Ryan asked.

"A 1997 Ford. Crown Victoria sedan. Four doors. White."

"Who saw you at the bar?"

"Who *saw* me there? You do realize it happened almost seventeen years ago, don't you? The bar doesn't even exist anymore!"

"Who did you talk to?"

"The bartender. I think her name was Shelley. But I haven't seen her in years."

"Anyone else?"

"Some of the boys from the area. You know, people who worked in the neighbourhood. I might be able to round up one or two, but I wouldn't expect anyone to remember that night. And there were a few tourists. I have no idea who they were. That's about it."

"If you'll write down the names of anyone you remember who might still be around, we'd appreciate it."

Dom rolled his eyes.

"You left around eleven?" Manziuk asked.

"Somewhere around there. Maybe ten or twenty minutes on either side. The hockey game was over, I'd had a few drinks, and I was sort of annoyed with Tony for standing me up. So I left."

"Where did you go?"

"I went to my car and drove home. I'd had a busy week and I had an open house on Saturday afternoon so I decided to get to bed early."

"Can anyone confirm that you went home?"

"I lived alone in a basement apartment. I can't say if the Baldwins, who owned the house and lived upstairs, heard me or not. They live in a home for seniors now. Mr. Baldwin had a stroke a few years back and can't really talk, and Mrs. Baldwin's health hasn't been well either. I drop in to see them every now and then, but I seriously doubt they'd remember whether or not they heard me come in that night. Half the time when I drop in I'm not sure they know who I am."

"Mr. Marino," Ryan said, "you don't seem very anxious to help us."

Dom started to say something, then sat down and put his elbows on the desk.

"It's not that I don't want to help you. It's just that I resent you coming here to give me the third degree. Me! Tony's best friend, who'd never have harmed a hair on his head! Who'd have gladly given my own life if it would have saved his!"

"Please understand that we have to look at anyone who gained by Tony's death."

"Gained? How did I gain?"

"If you were in love with Gina De Luca—"

"You've got to be joking! You think I killed Tony so I could marry Gina? That's ridiculous!"

"You *did* marry her."

Dom jumped up and walked around the desk. "I married her because it's what Tony would have wanted me to do. You know, just like in the Bible—in the Old Testament—where a brother would die and his younger brother would marry the widow in order to look after her. Well, that's what I did."

Ryan frowned. "Tony asked you to do that?"

"Of course not. He didn't know he was going to die, did he? No, it was Mama De Luca who showed me where it said that in the Bible. And it seemed right to me, and to Papa and Mama De Luca."

"What about your parents? How did they feel about it?"

Dom spit on the floor. "*My* parents? They have a place in Florida, near Tampa, and they live there for six months of the year. The rest of the time they're up at a cottage in the Muskokas. And they've got my two older brothers and three older sisters and their pack of kids to keep them busy. My parents don't care what I do. They never did. Even when I was growing up, I was at the De Lucas' house more than I was at my own. Tony was more my brother than my real brothers ever were."

Manziuk asked, "When you married her, did Gina know the part about the brother marrying the widow?"

Dom licked his lips. "In a way. But don't think I didn't want to marry her. I did. I'd been her friend for years, just like Tony, but it was Tony she fell in love with. When he was gone, well, I just took over looking out for her. Like a friend. She was still hoping Tony would come back. We all were. But by the time the court finally agreed that Tony was dead, it just seemed right to all of us to become a real family." Dom walked to the door. "Now, if you don't mind, I have no more time to answer stupid questions. I have work to do."

Emil Romano and his father Joe were both at their hardware store when Manziuk walked in. Ryan trailed after him.

When Manziuk said they'd like to speak with each of them alone, Emil complained, but Joe just said, "Emil, take a coffee break."

After glaring at his father, Emil led Manziuk and Ryan out the front door and down the street a block and a half to a small cafe with six red and yellow tables on the sidewalk in front. Each of the tables had four chairs and a red-and-yellow striped umbrella.

The sun was shining, and it was a perfect day to sit outside. A slight breeze served as a reminder that fall was just around the corner.

No other customers were sitting at the tables, so after they'd gone inside to pick up a latte and a dish of pistachio gelato for Emil, a black coffee for Manziuk, and a green tea for Ryan, they took their purchases outside.

When they were seated, Emil put a spoonful of his gelato in his mouth. "Aah… You don't know what you're missing."

Manziuk leaned forward and quietly said, "Emil, we're wondering if the person who killed Tony could have been someone who knew him. Maybe even someone close to him."

Emil set down his spoon and leaned toward Manziuk with narrowed eyes. "That's insane!"

"We have to rule out everyone we can. In order to do that, we need more details from you about that night."

Emil shook his head. "I already told you everything. We closed the store at nine, my father left, and I stayed late to work on some things."

"What things?"

He swallowed another spoonful of gelato before pushing his chair back and crossing his legs. "As a sideline, we do a lot of bike repairs. I had a couple of bikes a customer had brought in. I'd promised to have them ready by Saturday, but I hadn't had time to work on them because we'd had a busy day on Friday. So I decided to work on them that night while I wouldn't be interrupted."

Ryan said, "You told us earlier that you'd considered joining Tony and Dom at the bar."

"So I did. But I decided the bikes were more important."

"Did you phone your wife or anyone else? Or did you see anyone?" Manziuk asked. "Or might someone have seen you through the doors?"

"I didn't phone anybody and nobody phoned me. I turned off the front lights and worked in the back with the door shut because I didn't want somebody knocking on the door thinking I'd open up for them. That's happened before."

"Did your father know you were working on the bikes?"

Emil shrugged. "I don't know. Maybe. But I might have decided to work on them after he left."

He glared at them. "Since I didn't know I'd need an alibi, I didn't plan ahead. The only reason I remember any of this is because Tony disappeared. We talked about that evening more than a few times."

"Do you remember what the problems were with the bikes you fixed?"

"You've got to be kidding! I've fixed thousands of bikes. No, I don't remember exactly what I did that night. Likely something to do with the brakes, the tires, or the chains. Those are the most common problems."

Ryan said, "Do you remember whose bikes they were?"

"As if!" Emil shook his head. "And no, we don't keep our records for seventeen years."

Manziuk said, "Can you think of anyone—anyone at all—who might have resented Tony or had a grudge of some sort against him?"

"I didn't follow him around all day. He worked, he played soccer, he talked to his neighbours, he went to Mass, he took his kids to the park—for all I know there were a dozen people who didn't like him for one reason or another, but I can't think of anyone in particular, no."

There was a moment of silence, and then Emil gave them a puzzled look. "Why would you think the person who killed him knew him?"

"Because," Ryan said, "it seems odd to us that someone with no connection to him, who likely wouldn't be a suspect if his body had been found back then, would go to all the effort of taking his body deep into the woods in the Don Valley to bury it."

Emil frowned. "I—yeah, I get what you're saying." He thought for a moment. "So you think you'll be able to find out who did this?"

"We're going to do our best," Manziuk said. "We don't give up easily."

"If you think of anything—anything at all," Ryan said, "let us know." She handed Emil a card.

He put the card in his pocket, finished his gelato, picked up his coffee, and walked back to the hardware store.

A few minutes after Emil went into the store, Joe Romano came out and walked down to sit at the table with Manziuk and Ryan. While Manziuk repeated what they'd told Emil about needing more information, Ryan went inside to buy Joe a cup of black coffee and a Sicilian cannoli that made Manziuk's mouth water.

"As I said already," Joe mumbled, his mouth full, "I left shortly after we closed at nine and I walked down to a pub to meet some friends. Emil was still in the store. He said he had some things he wanted to finish repairing. Bikes, I think."

After a moment, Manziuk said, "Mr. Romano, how did you feel about having Tony as your son-in-law?"

Joe shrugged. "Good. I felt good. His parents were friends of ours, and Gina and Tony kind of grew up together and started dating in high school. They were happy together and they gave me two amazing grandkids."

"Can you think of anyone who might have had a grudge against Tony?"

"Nah. Tony was a good guy. Not the kind to make enemies."

Ryan asked, "Do you think he could have been playing around?"

"What? You mean another woman? Nothing I ever saw to make me think that."

"If you had heard something, what would you have done about it?"

Joe crossed his arms. His voice trembled with emotion as he said, "If you ask any of my family members or my friends, you will learn that I have never raised my hand in anger to a single person." He leaned forward. "I'll tell you why. My parents, when I was growing up, they fought all the time.

And I mean literally fought. My mother would hit my father and he would hit her. And when we children didn't toe the line, one or the other of them would hit us. I left home when I was fifteen, and the day I walked away, I made a vow that I would never raise my hand in anger toward another person."

After a long moment, Manziuk said, "What would you have done if you'd heard that Tony was involved with another woman?"

"I would have told him what I'd heard and asked for an explanation. And if he said it was true, I would have called for a family meeting with everyone there to discuss it: Gina, Emil, Tony's parents… the whole family. That's how we do things. We talk them out."

Lee Romano answered the doorbell wearing a sleeveless blue maxi dress and gold sandals. Her long, honey-blonde hair flowed around her shoulders. "Well, this *is* a surprise," she said. "I didn't expect to see either of you again."

"May we come in for a few minutes?" Manziuk asked.

"Of course." She stepped back to let them in.

Ryan looked around in astonishment. From the outside, the house, which was in the Annex area northeast of Little Italy, was just another narrow three-storey brick building on a small plot of land. But inside, it was spectacular. The front hallway was large and airy; the stairs leading to the second floor were a light oak with soft white carpet runners. The walls were covered with pale cream wallpaper that sparkled with gold where the sun hit it. A narrow white cabinet held the only bit of colour—a tall red vase holding a small bouquet of yellow flowers with dark green leaves.

To the right, a wide arch led to an airy living room. As in the hallway, there was a lot of pale cream with just a few accents—pictures, pillows, and throws—in shades of yellow, red, and green.

"Like it?" Lee asked with a twinkle in her eyes.

"I love it!" Ryan replied. "I live in a narrow house like this, but it looks so crowded and messy even when it's tidy."

"Less is more," Lee said. "Go through it and keep only what you really love. Get rid of the rest. You'll feel so much better."

Since Jacquie shared the house with four other women, it wasn't that simple, but she filed away the idea for future reference.

"Come in and sit down," Lee said. "I was just going to have some iced tea. May I offer you some? It's already made."

Ryan glanced at Manziuk, who nodded. "Yes, please."

While Lee went to get the tea, Manziuk and Ryan sat down on the pale cream chesterfield in the living room.

"I love this room," Ryan said.

"It looks as if no one lives here."

"True. I love it."

Lee returned with tall glasses of iced tea and settled down on a large ottoman. "Now, how can I help you? Have you learned something more about Tony's death?"

Manziuk said, "Now that we know for certain the remains are those of Tony De Luca, we're trying to discover what happened to him."

Lee smiled. "You mean you're looking for someone to blame. Do you really think it was murder? Might it not have been an accident?"

"Someone buried the body."

Lee looked at the glass of tea she was holding. "Yes, but—I guess I just can't believe it. Everyone liked Tony."

"You can't think of a single person who might have had a grudge against him?"

She shook her head.

Ryan said, "You're a woman, and you must have been around him a fair bit. Did he show interest in you, or in other women?"

Lee pursed her lips, as if her drink were sour. "Tony was my brother-in-law, so, yes, I was around him. But he never showed any interest in me, other than what you'd expect from family. And as far as I could tell, he never even saw any women other than Gina."

Manziuk cleared his throat. "Do you have anything to add to what you said before about being at home the night he disappeared?"

"No."

"Did you talk to anyone that evening?"

"Not that I can recall. But it was a long time ago, and—" she shrugged "—as I told you, I was tired after working a twelve-hour shift, and I had a couple of glasses of wine. I might have forgotten something."

"Did you ever see Tony arguing with someone? Your husband, perhaps? Dom? Tony's father?"

She raised her eyebrows. "Arguing? Of course. I mean, nobody agrees all the time. But arguing is a broad term. I never saw him fight with anyone. Just disagree about things like who would win soccer games. Nothing important. Tony wasn't the kind of person who fought people. And neither are Emil or Dom or Mario or Joe. You're going to have to come up with another angle. I can't seriously believe anybody who knew him would intentionally kill Tony."

They made it to Raphael's barber shop just before he closed the door at 5 p.m.

"Ah, my friends from the Homicide Squad," Raphael said. He looked over at the other barber, who had been sweeping up while Raphael tidied the shelf next to his barber chair. "George, you are in exalted company."

George, an older man with ebony skin, a closely-shaved head, and muscular arms, looked anything but impressed.

"We have a few more questions for you," Ryan said to Raphael.

"Of course you do." Raphael turned to George. "You can go. I'll see you bright and early on Monday."

With a quick look at Ryan, George grabbed a backpack from behind the front desk and scurried out of the shop.

"Has George been in trouble?" Manziuk asked casually.

Raphael laughed. "Not recently. But he has a strong dislike of anyone in authority. And not without good reason. He's been carded one too many times. Now, what can I do for you?"

Ryan said, "Now that we know the remains we found belong to Tony De Luca, we're talking to the people closest to him again. Looking for any leads we can find. We dropped by to see if you've thought of anything you might have forgotten to tell us about that evening? Or about any enemies Tony might have had? Trouble he'd been in?"

"Afraid I can't help you." Raphael licked his lips. "You know, I would if I could. As I told you, Tony was a nice guy and I have only good things to say about him. I'd like to have the lout who killed Tony in my back room for a few minutes so I could show him what I think of him."

Manziuk said, "Did you know any women who might have been attracted to Tony? Someone who might have had a boyfriend or husband who was angry?"

Raphael put his hands on his hips. "How many times do I have to tell you? No! You'd be better to spend your time looking through the arrest sheets from back then. I'd be willing to lay down a few grand that it was nothing more than a robbery that went wrong. Tony was young and in good shape from playing soccer. I doubt that he'd have taken kindly to being robbed, you know? I guarantee you that's what happened."

"Could you and Tony have left together," Ryan said, "and walked to his house? Or maybe you drove him home and stopped to talk something over?"

Raphael just stared at her. "Now why would I want to do that? If I'd needed to talk to him, I'd have done it right here. And besides, I don't own a car now and I didn't own one then either. I ride a bicycle. Been doing it for years. It's how I keep in shape."

"So that night, Tony left at ten past nine and you left a few minutes later?" Manziuk asked.

"That's right."

"Where did you keep your bike?"

"In the back room. But—wait a minute. Now that I think about it, I didn't have my bike that night. My wife had ridden down with me that morning and we'd left our bikes with Emil to have some things done. We were supposed to get them back the next day. My wife went home by streetcar in the morning and I went home the same way after I left at nine."

"And did you get the bikes the next day?"

Raphael paused, obviously trying to dredge up a memory. "No, we didn't," he said slowly. "When I went to pick them up, they weren't ready, and we didn't get them until the next week. Wednesday, I think it was. As I recall, I think Emil planned to work on them early that Saturday morning and with Tony missing, he forgot all about them."

Raphael walked over to pick up the broom George had set down. "Now, you got any other questions, you better ask them quick. I need to finish closing and get home. My wife invited her mother over for supper tonight, and the old biddy gets crotchety if we don't eat on time."

"What a waste of a day!" Ryan said as they drove back to police headquarters.

Manziuk who was driving, said, "Pretty much. Other than Felicia's memory fragment, which may or may not be accurate, I'm not sure we got anything useful."

"Well, I guess we learned a few things. Dom can get pretty in your face when he feels attacked. And Emil gets like a stone wall. Either of them would be capable of defending themselves or someone they cared about."

"True, but from what we've learned about Tony, he'd be unlikely to attack them, and there's no one they'd need to protect from him."

"Yeah." There was a long silence, before Ryan added, "Maybe Ident will find something."

"I hope so."

"At least we're getting a normal evening off."

"Right."

"Tomorrow's Sunday. Do we get it off, too?"

"I think so. But we'll need to figure out a new line of attack. Right now, all we have to go on is the vague memory of a six-year-old. That won't impress Seldon at all."

By 6:15 Monday morning, Felicia Marino was at the parking lot nearest to the trail that led to the crime scene in the woods. She'd agreed to meet Evan there at six-thirty, but she'd awakened early and decided to get up rather than lie in bed trying to get back to sleep. Now, instead of standing around in the parking lot, she sent a text to Evan and started jogging on her own.

When she reached the crime scene area, she checked the live trap. It was empty. So no dog again today. Maybe Sam Benson was right. Apparently he thought the dog probably wasn't a stray but just a dog that lived in the neighbourhood and just happened to be in the woods the day Evan had seen it. Evan wasn't sure.

Felicia smiled. She loved that Evan was so concerned about a dog he'd only seen once. He was so unlike any of the guys she knew. None of them would be willing to use their free time to search for a stray dog. But that wasn't the only thing. Evan didn't seem in the least bit threatened by her. Also unlike most of the guys she knew. They all seemed to want her to act as if they were smarter than she was even when it was obvious to everyone that they weren't. With Evan, she could be completely herself. It was a novel experience.

She shook her head. She wasn't here to think about Evan. Or to check the dog trap. Ever since she'd first heard that human remains that had been found were those of her father, she'd had a feeling that there was something—a clue of some sort—that she could find if only she knew where to look—and if she didn't give up. This was a perfect time for her to look around.

She picked up a long stick and began walking slowly around the ground next to the crime scene tape, peering behind every rock and using the stick to part the bushes so she could check under them.

About ten minutes into her search, something caught her eye. A glint. She used her stick to move the branches of a bush, and then gasped.

Reaching into her pocket for the latex gloves she'd brought just in case, she put them on. She took out a small marker she'd made, with a 1 on it, and squatted down to set it next to the item. Then she took pictures from different angles, just the way she'd seen them do on CSI. Only then did she reach carefully for the item and very gently lift it up. If it had resisted, she'd have stopped. But it came away easily. It was a gold chain, and it had a large gold cross attached to it. She put it into a small plastic bag she'd brought for that purpose. Then, her heart beating fast, she looked for a place to sit down.

Seeing a largish rock a little farther into the trees, she started walking toward it. She had reached the rock and had turned to sit down when something on the ground about twenty feet in front of her caught her eye.

She made sure she'd turned off the clicking sound her camera made, then used it to magnify what she was seeing. It looked like a small greyish-brown animal, curled in a ball on some leaves that had drifted into an indentation in the ground. She could see the puppy's side rising and falling with each breath. She could see each rib, too. It had to be the one Evan had been trying to catch. Apparently the pup had been smart enough not to go in the live trap, even though it must have wanted the food.

Much as she wanted to focus on the chain, Felicia knew that catching the puppy was more urgent. She quickly sent a text.

> Evan, I see him. He's not in the trap though. He's curled up under a bush. Can u come?

> R u serious? 10 minutes away. Don't go near him. Just in case.

> How do you know it's a him? It might be a her. :)

> Well, wait till I get there 2 find out. :)

> Hurry!

Poor little thing, Felicia thought. *I'm sorry you've had such a bad time. But I'm glad you were here, because otherwise who knows when we'd have found my daddy?*

The dog was still sleeping, and Felicia hadn't moved, when Evan slipped quietly through the trees to stand beside her.

Where? he mimed.

She pointed, and he nodded, then whispered in her ear, "I need you to leave us for now. You can watch, but go quietly around the trees so you're out of his line of vision. I want him to only see me. And don't say anything or come out until I tell you it's okay."

Felicia did as requested, and was soon peeking out from behind a tree some distance away. She could see both Evan and the dog.

Evan moved to within about ten feet of the dog, then sat down on the ground. He carefully took off his backpack and set it gently on the ground, then reached in and took out a plastic container with several slices of cold pepperoni pizza. Then he broke off and tossed a few pieces of the pizza in front of him, some close and some further away.

Then he carefully pulled a small bag of potato chips from his backpack, and carefully cut the bag open with the pair of scissors on his Swiss Army Knife. His head down, he began crinkling the bag and smacking his lips.

The little dog jerked awake at the first rustle of the chips bag. It jumped up and looked around wildly to see where the noise was coming from.

Without looking in the dog's direction, Evan dropped some of the chips and picked them up one by one, eating them as if they were the best food he'd ever had. Then he broke off more pieces of the pizza and dropped them onto the ground. Every so often, he yawned and shut his eyes, or coughed and leaned back.

The pup watching closely, its body tense, ready to run. But Felicia thought curiosity, or perhaps the smell of the pizza, was proving more powerful than fear, at least for the moment.

As Evan kept dropping chips and picking them up to pretend to put them in his mouth, the dog took a step forward, its eyes on the nearest piece of pizza on the ground about four feet in front of him.

After a few minutes, the puppy moved closer. When Evan paid no attention, but kept on yawning and pretending to eat the chips, it got down on its stomach, still tensed.

Evan ate some more chips, crinkling the bag loudly. Then he tossed a few pieces of the pizza about halfway between himself and dog.

"You're safe, little one," he said softly. "Nothing at all to worry about."

The dog pricked up its ears and stared at him.

"Here you go," Evan said in the same soft voice. A piece of pizza landed just a foot or so in front of the dog.

With a quick movement, the dog darted forward, grabbed the pizza, and moved back.

Still keeping his head down, Evan picked a chip off the ground and ate it, licking his lips and saying, "Mmm, that's good!"

The dog wriggled forward and grabbed the piece of pizza next closest to him. But this time it didn't move back. After swallowing, it moved a few inches further and grabbed the next piece.

Evan continued eating and speaking in a soothing voice. "Good dog. You're smart, aren't you? Everything's going to be just fine." The next piece of pizza landed just a few feet in front of Evan's crossed legs.

Eyes on Evan, the dog stood up, moved cautiously toward the food, and gulped it down.

"Good dog," Evan said. "Good boy." Careful not to look into the dog's eyes, he held out a large piece of pizza.

The dog's eyes were on Evan's face as it stepped forward and carefully accepted the food.

Evan kept his hand out so that the dog could sniff it.

After a few moments, the dog lay down, head next to Evan's hand. Then its tongue came out and licked the hand.

"Good boy," Evan said.

The pup rolled over so that Evan could rub its stomach.

"Yep, you are definitely a boy," Evan said, grinning at Felicia. A moment later, the dog was snuggled in his arms, licking his face.

Evan fed the pup the last pieces of the pizza.

While it was eating, he reached down with his right hand and picked up the slip lead he'd brought. It was basically a collar and leash in one piece.

He put the collar over the dog's head before saying softly, "Felicia, come out very slowly and speak quietly."

She did as told.

Aside from pricking up its ears and staring at her, the dog accepted Felicia's presence.

After she gave it a couple of potato chips, it even sniffed her hand and let her pat its stomach.

"Now what do we do?" she asked.

"We take him to the clinic where I work and give him a good bath, a checkup, healthier food, and a lot of cuddling."

"How will you get him there?"

"The best thing would be for you to drive us there in my car so I can hold him. Then, when he's settled in, I'll drive you back for your car."

She thought for a second. "I'd rather drive you in my car."

"Are you sure? He's pretty dirty."

"I have a blanket in the trunk we can put on the seat. I'd prefer not to drive a car I don't know."

"No problem. Also, that works better because you can leave any time and I can have someone from the clinic drive me back to get my car."

She got up. "You bring the dog; I'll bring the trap."

"Can you manage it?"

"Just tell me how to collapse it."

As she started to go for the trap, Felicia remembered the baggie in her pocket. "No, wait. I have to show you something first." She pulled the plastic bag from her pocket and held it out. "Evan, I think this might have belonged to my dad. I found it this morning in a small bush on this side of the crime scene tape. I think I'd better call the police."

As Evan, still holding the pup, stood up to get a closer look, they heard a rustling noise and a short man in a brown hoodie and khaki shorts rushed toward them and snapped a picture of Felicia holding out the chain.

SIX

"Hey," Evan yelled. "What are you doing? This is a crime scene!"

"Not on this side of the tape, it isn't." The man was moving away, but he stopped to snap a picture of Evan and the pup. "Don't worry. I'm a reporter. This is my job."

"You're the one who tried to follow me the other day," Evan said. "What's your name? You can't use those pictures. You don't have permission!"

The man laughed. "You can read the story online."

Evan handed the dog to Felicia and chased him, but the man had a bicycle propped against a tree near the trail, and he got away easily. Evan came back to find Felicia sitting on the rock petting the dog and talking to it.

"Sorry to dump him on you," Evan said. "Is he okay?"

"Yes, he seems to like me."

"He'd be pretty silly if he didn't."

Felicia smiled. "Well, thank you."

"He had a bike." Evan took a few deep breaths. "Guess I'm not as in as good shape as I thought I was. Not that I know what I'd have done with him if I'd caught him." He flopped down on the ground beside Felicia. "Did you call the cops?"

"Constable Ryan gave me her number, so I texted her. She said she'd call Inspector Manziuk and Special Constable Ford. She said they'll be here soon and not to move or touch anything else."

"Good. I guess I should let Constable Benson know we have the dog. He wanted to be the first to know. Even came out here with me to check the trap the last two nights."

"Do you think the dog is okay?"

"Hard to tell, but he looks all right to me. Aside from the dirt and the burrs and not getting enough to eat, that is. But I can't tell for sure without doing a thorough check. He might have fleas or any number of things we can't see."

She made a face. "I hope he doesn't."

"Let me take him."

Felicia gave the dog back to Evan. "The sneaky reporter guy took his picture."

"Yeah. Maybe if it does get in a paper, his owner will see it and come get him."

"What if he has no owner?"

"I don't know. I'll try to find a home for him, I guess. Assuming he's healthy and all."

"Poor little guy." Felicia's eyes filled with tears.

"He'll be okay."

"I know you won't let anything bad happen to him."

"I'll do my best."

"I know you will."

Felicia slipped off the rock onto the ground next to Evan and leaned her head on his shoulder.

As Evan moved the puppy to his left arm and put his right arm around Felicia's waist, he asked, "Are you okay?"

"I suddenly felt afraid. What do you think it means that I found the chain here? I thought the police searched all around here. Why didn't they find it? And how did it get into a bush? It doesn't make any sense. Maybe I've watched too many forensic shows, but I think it means something. Something bad."

As Felicia gave the chain to Manziuk, she said, "It's the same as the one in the picture Mom showed you a couple of days ago, isn't it?"

"It certainly seems to be."

"But if it had been buried here for almost seventeen years, it wouldn't be in a bush, would it? And I think it would look dirtier or more tarnished or something."

"We'll have to check with a jeweller, but I tend to agree with you."

Ford said, "It depends on how much of it is gold and how much is alloys. The gold would stay pretty well the same, but an alloy might rust or get tarnished. However," —he paused for dramatic effect— "that's not the most interesting thing. My team went over all this ground the first day. Not only the area we put the tape around, but this whole area where the chain was found and further out. If this chain had been here that day, we'd have found it."

"How can you be certain of that?" Evan said. "People make mistakes all the time."

"I'm not saying we're always a hundred percent perfect, but in this case, I'm *very* certain. Constable Kelly and I searched this area and I actually remember looking in that clump of brush myself. The chain wasn't here."

Felicia's eyes seemed to grow larger. "But that means—"

Evan's jaw dropped. "Do you really think someone put it here recently? But why?"

"Good question," Manziuk said. "The obvious reason would be that whoever had it was afraid that we might get a search warrant and find it."

Felicia said, "But why would anyone keep something that would incriminate him?"

"Several possible reasons," Ryan said. "He wanted a souvenir. He was afraid of destroying it because of its religious connections. Guilt because he knew of its meaning to the family. Wanting to cash in on it because it was gold. Or simply not knowing what to do with it."

"But to put it *here*?" Felicia said. "That makes no sense. It's as if he wanted our family to have it."

"It's possible," Manziuk said. "Which makes me think it might have been kept because of guilt. And that's why it was put here and not buried or dropped in a lake somewhere."

"What will you do now?" Felicia asked.

"Check it carefully for fingerprints and anything else that might be on it," Manziuk said. "Have a jeweller examine it and the pictures, and determine whether or not it really is your father's. And then try to figure out who put it here."

Felicia brought her hands up as if in prayer, clasping them under her chin. "You think it was someone in our family, don't you? Or someone close to us?"

"Yes, we think it was," Manziuk said. "Can the two of you keep this to yourselves for a day or two?"

Felicia took a deep breath. "I can't believe that someone I know could have killed my dad."

"I hope it wasn't," Manziuk said, "but it's looking more and more as if it was."

She stepped back. "You really want me to pretend that none of this happened?"

"For a short time."

Felicia licked her lips and looked at Evan, who was standing next to her, still holding the puppy.

"I won't say anything."

Felicia took a deep breath. "All right. I won't even tell Mom or Bruno."

Looking into Ryan's eyes, she said, "You'll let me know the minute you find out anything? Please?"

"We'll keep you informed," Ryan said.

Felicia shivered. "All of a sudden this is really scary."

Evan looked at Manziuk. "If you have no objections, I'll take the pup to the clinic where I work and we'll give him a thorough checkup and look after him."

"That's fine with me," Manziuk said. "I don't think he can tell us anything more."

Special Constable Benson had been listening and making notes. "I need a picture of you with the dog, Evan. People have been asking about it."

"You have the first ones I took. Can you wait until we get him cleaned up?"

"I suppose. But I need it as soon as possible."

"As soon as he's had a bath, I'll have someone take a picture and email it to you."

"I guess that'll do."

Felicia looked at Evan. "I'll pay for whatever care he needs. I owe him a lot."

Evan smiled. "We'll work something out."

As they turned to leave, she added, "We'll have to think of a name for him."

Sam Benson returned to police headquarters to work on his news release about the finding of the dog. He wanted to say something about the chain, too, but that would have to wait.

The part of the job he loved best was being able to release good news. There was always too much of the other kind.

Manziuk and Ryan had gone to his office to wait for the forensic results.

Manziuk sat down and then stretched out in his chair. "I could really do without these early morning alarms."

Ryan sat on the other chair. "Me, too. I have my morning workout routine, and I hate when I can't do it."

"I just like getting that last hour of undisturbed sleep."

"How was your day off yesterday?"

"Okay. I got to spend some time with my wife. I'd hoped to see my son, too, but he had an ultimate tournament this weekend."

"Ultimate? You mean fighting?"

"No. They play it with a disc. What most people call a Frisbee, except that's a brand."

"I don't get it. Is it just a couple of people playing catch, like you see at the parks?"

"No, it's a real game. There are teams all over the world. Michael started playing this summer and he's really enjoying it. He had a tournament in Kitchener this weekend. Now that I think about it, we should have driven out yesterday to watch." He looked over at her. "How was your day?"

"Oh, just great if you like sharing a house with people who aren't speaking to each other."

"What's up?"

"My mother, my aunt, and my cousin all want to modernize Grams' kitchen. But Grams says no way. And she owns the house. We're basically squatters. And because we all work and she's at home, she does most of the cooking."

"So what's the problem? I mean, why does everyone else want to change the kitchen if it belongs to her and she's happy as it is?"

"Well, really, they're right. It should be redone. I'm not sure anything's been changed since they bought the house back in the mid-sixties. I guess there's been a new stove and fridge, and a microwave. But probably nothing else. She doesn't even have a dishwasher. But I think redoing it would be really expensive. They'd likely have to rip it apart. I don't blame Gram for not wanting to do it."

"Tricky," Manziuk said.

"Very. Which is why I didn't totally mind getting the call early this morning so I didn't have to see everyone at breakfast."

Constable Ari Bixby had dusted the chain for fingerprints. He found a few smudges and used lifting tape to capture them. He placed the tape on three by five cards that he put into paper envelopes, sealed, and wrote on.

He then examined every link of the chain, as well the cross, with a strong magnifying glass. Using tweezers, he picked up the dirt and small pieces of vegetation he found and put them into small paper bags that he labelled and sealed. On the link that joined the cross to the chain, he found a small whitish speck. He got out a couple of cotton swabs and carefully wiped up the substance and placed it and the swabs in a sealed and labelled plastic bag. Then he did a last check to see if there was anything else before putting the chain into a paper bag and giving it to Ford to pass on to Manziuk.

Once they had the chain, Manziuk and Ryan drove to the store of a jeweller the police sometimes used for assessing the value of items. He was busy when they entered, but as soon as his customer left, he put on latex gloves and picked up the chain.

"This is a crucifix," he said. "Both the chain and the cross are fourteen karat gold. Very nice design. Classic. A very simple cross, but a good size. One a man would wear with pleasure. I'd value it at between three hundred fifty and four hundred dollars."

"Would you say it's been buried in the ground in a wooded area for nearly seventeen years?"

"Like this? Or has it been cleaned?"

"We removed a few bits of dirt and vegetation, but otherwise just like this. I can show you photos of it exactly as it was when it was found."

After looking closely at the photos, the jeweller said, "Well, the gold would stay quite shiny if that's what you mean. It's good quality. But I'd think there would be a bit of tarnishing. And if it was really buried in the ground, without protection, for all that time, there should be dirt caked on it, making it look a lot grungier, as my daughter would say." He looked up. "Looks to me as if someone dropped it into some dirt to make it look as if it had been buried."

Back at police headquarters, Manziuk met with Superintendent Cliff Seldon. After outlining what they'd discovered, he summed up his report with, "Looks to me as if someone is scared."

Seldon said, "Do you have a primary suspect?"

"Not really. Based on the few interviews the police had seventeen years ago, and what we've found out recently, the obvious persons of interest are his wife, his best friend—who by the way married the widow, his boss, or a member of the wife's family."

"Wait. His best friend married his wife?"

"Yes."

"That sounds to me like a good place to start."

"That's what we think, too."

"It's going to get messy."

"I know. And I'd like to keep the details out of the press as long as we can."

"I'll talk to Benson and see if we can figure out a way to make the press happy without giving them any details."

"I think he plans to use the dog angle."

"I'm a cat person myself," Seldon said, "but many people do like dogs."

After leaving Seldon, Manziuk went to his office. Ryan had picked up salads so they could have lunch while figuring out their next moves.

After he'd brought her up to date as to his meeting with Seldon, Ryan said, "So when do I get included?"

"What?"

"You always talk to Seldon and then tell me what was said. When do I become part of the briefing? You know, instead of the designated lunch gofer?"

"I—uh—I don't know. Woody never went to the briefings."

"I know you worked with Woody for a very long time and the two of you developed ways of doing things. But, as we've discussed in the past, I'm not Woody."

"No, you're not." After a second, he said. "I'm an inspector and you're a constable. It's normal for higher-ranking officers to be the ones who report to Seldon."

"I still have to write reports. And we usually plan together," she said. "I thought the idea was that we work together as a team."

Manziuk stared at her. He had no answer.

Ryan's phone buzzed. "Saved by the bell," she said before answering. She listened for a minute and then closed her phone. "Ford and Benson are on their way here. Something just came up, and Ford says we aren't going to be happy."

Benson followed Ford into the office and handed his tablet to Manziuk. "I phoned Evan McEwan and asked him if he'd talked to any reporters. He said no. But then he remembered that some guy showed up this morning and took a couple of pictures just as Felicia was showing him the chain. Evan said they told him he wasn't supposed to take pictures, but he said he was a reporter, and just laughed and took off on a bike. Evan apologized that they'd forgotten to mention it in the excitement over finding the chain and the dog."

"Anyway, the damage is done," Ford said. "Just read the stories. The first one isn't a big deal, but the second might be a problem."

Ryan jumped up and came around the desk to read over Manziuk's shoulder.

The first story was accompanied by a photo of an angry-looking Evan holding the dog.

Who killed Tony De Luca?

by Questioner

Stray dog leads to the discovery of a body

On the evening of October 18, 1999, Tony De Luca, a family man and barber who lived and worked in the area of Toronto known as Little Italy, said good-bye to his boss, walked out of the barber shop where he'd worked for nearly eight years, and stepped into oblivion.

For nearly seventeen years, Tony De Luca was considered missing. Like thousands of other Canadians, he was a statistic; someone who didn't exist, and yet did.

His wife Gina was left with two young children and the aftermath of not knowing.; the need to make decisions and to struggle with necessities such as access to her husband's bank account.

It wasn't until 2005 that Tony was officially declared dead. Not that everyone was convinced he *was* dead. His wife and family believed he was, but many people, including the police, believed Tony had walked away from his life in Toronto into a new life, a new name, and the arms of another woman.

Eventually, even Gina moved on. In 2007, she married Dom Marino, Tony's best friend. Two years later, Dom adopted her children and they took his last name. The last trappings of Tony De Luca's life were gone. Dom moved into the De Luca home, where Tony's parents also lived, in a basement apartment. Dom had taken the place of their son.

And then, a week ago, a stray dog led Evan McEwan, a jogger and veterinarian-in-training, to a clearing in the woods of the Don Valley off Bayview Avenue and brought the story of Tony De Luca back to life.

Sitting in the clearing was a skull. Nearby, police found the rest of the skeleton. With the help of forensic anthropologist Dr. Suzy Wong, it took only a couple of days to identify the skeleton as that of Tony De Luca.

His death has been officially ruled a homicide.

Now, the only question left to answer is who killed Tony De Luca and left his body to rot in the Don Valley?

It's not hard to see who benefited most from Tony's death.

The second story was accompanied by a photo of a surprised Felicia, her hands holding up a plastic bag which held something that looked like a chain.

Murdered Man's Daughter Finds a Clue?
By Questioner

What is she holding?

The police said they made a thorough search of the entire area where the body of Tony De Luca, who had been missing since October 18, 1999, was found last Tuesday. But early this morning, Tony's daughter decided to conduct her own search. And she obviously found something of importance. It's hard to tell what the object is, and police refuse to share the information, but if you examine this picture, you'll see it looks like some kind of chain or necklace.

What does this discovery mean?

When I left, the police were doing another search of the site. Hopefully a more thorough one than the first.

Stay tuned for more revelations.

"Oh, that's just great!" Ryan said.

"Both stories are all over the Internet," Ford said, "and I doubt if we can contain them."

"Could he be sued?" Ryan asked. "He more or less accuses Dom Marino of killing Tony."

"Not in so many words," Benson said. "I doubt if you'd get a legit lawyer to take the case."

"The real problem," Ford said, "is that he makes us look incompetent. And the only way we can refute it is to let people know we suspect someone put the chain there after we searched."

"Which we can't do," Manziuk said.

Benson sighed. "Which we can't do."

"What can we do?" Ford asked.

Manziuk stood up and the others moved back to give him room. Looking at Ford, he said, "Can you track this Questioner guy down and keep him from posting any other information we don't want released?"

"Already working on it. We're also sifting through every possible bit of info that could help us identify the person who brought the chain."

Manziuk turned back to Benson, "Can you update Seldon? And send out the story of the dog that you were going to release?"

"The story's ready. I sent a note to Evan and he said we'll have a picture in a few minutes."

"Okay, get the official release out ASAP and try to bury this one."

"I'll do my best."

Manziuk began packing up to leave.

After Felicia dropped Evan off at the veterinary clinic where he was working for the summer, he'd taken "before" pictures of the dog, then scanned it to see if it had a microchip, which it didn't. He'd then checked to see if it had fleas, removed a bunch of burrs, twigs, and other remnants of nature from its fur, and checked it for obvious injuries.

Next, he watched one of the veterinarians from the clinic do a more thorough evaluation.

"I think he's okay," she said at last. "He's underfed, but he's not starving. I'd say he's between three and four months old. If we can find his owner and learn what shots he's had, that would be good. Otherwise, keep an eye on him and make sure he's gaining weight and so forth. As for breed, my guess would be a mixture of either border terrier or Jack Russell terrier with some dachshund and possibly one or more other breeds."

After giving him a bath, Evan took a few "after" pictures of the dog, had one of the technicians take a couple of photos of him with the dog, and sent them to Benson.

Here you go. If you can add something about the dog's owner getting in touch with us at the clinic, that would be great.

When Felicia had dropped them off at the clinic, Evan had promised to keep her informed, so he texted her and sent her the same pictures. She responded almost immediately.

How about Buddy? I've always liked that name for a dog.

Have you ever had a dog?

No. My mom doesn't like dogs. She says they're too much trouble. One of my biggest frustrations. She doesn't like cats either. Or hamsters. We did have a turtle for a while.

Evan looked down at the dog, sitting on the floor wagging his tail and gazing up at Evan with adoring eyes. The dog raised a paw and placed it on Evan's foot. Evan responded by reaching down to pick him up. "Buddy," Evan said, "I have no idea where this is going, but I think you just might be my good luck charm."

Gina put her hand over her mouth. "It's Tony's crucifix," she said. "I'm positive." She jumped up and ran to her photo albums, returning in a couple of minutes with a picture of a shirtless Tony holding a soccer trophy in the air and wearing his chain. "You can see it clearly here."

Manziuk took the picture and held it close. "Yes, it's a match," he said.

"I don't understand. I thought you said before that it hadn't been found?"

"It was found this morning, near where we found his body. Caught in a bush."

"But—how could it be there?"

"We think someone put it there in the last few days."

Gina put both hands to her face. "Oh, no! Oh, no!"

Dom was out of his office, but they were able to catch him at a house he was showing to some clients. They waited for his clients to leave, and then handed him the bag containing the chain.

"I don't understand. Where did you get this? You said it was missing."

They told him what had happened and he leaned against his car, his back turned to them.

"Mr. Marino?" Manziuk said.

"Just give me a minute."

"All right."

He took a few deep breaths before facing them. "Have you shown it to Gina?"

"Yes."

"It's his, isn't it?"

"If not, it's a perfect match."

"I don't know what to say. I didn't put it there if that's what you're thinking."

"Do you have any idea who might have?"

"None."

"None?" Ryan asked skeptically.

"No ideas I don't find impossible to believe."

"Mr. Marino," Manziuk said, "you do realize you're the obvious suspect, don't you?"

He looked down and kicked at a pebble on the grass. After a moment, he looked up. "Look, if you want me to take a lie-detector test, I will. But I'll be totally honest with you. I've never said this to anybody, but all these years, even though I didn't hurt him myself, I've always felt as if it was my fault."

"How is that?"

"Every single day, I wake up feeling guilty because I'm so glad he disappeared." When they didn't respond, he went on. "You were right. I was in love with Gina from the day I first realized girls could be more than friends you joked around with and teased. Only it was Tony she was interested in, and he was my best friend. Honestly, I'd never have done anything to hurt him, but when he disappeared, after Gina turned to me, I realized I was glad. And when I realized that, I felt so much guilt—as if I'd somehow caused him to leave.

"As for what happened, I honestly thought he'd gone off and killed himself, knowing I'd take care of Gina and the kids. And that it was somehow my fault.

"Discovering that someone killed him—well, the truth is, it's a relief. I don't have to keep blaming myself. But I really don't know who did it. I don't even want to make a guess."

Manziuk and Ryan were on the way to Joe and Emil Romano's hardware store when Ryan's phone buzzed. Since she was driving, Manziuk answered it.

"Inspector, this is Raphael Chiarelli. Your partner left me a card when you were here the first day, and I kept it just in case I ever needed a cop to fix a ticket for me." When Manziuk didn't respond, he said, "I'm joking, Inspector."

Manziuk said, "Did you think of something?"

"Sort of. Likely nothing that has anything to do with it, but you said to tell you anything."

"We appreciate it."

"Okay, so here's the thing. After you left here Saturday, I got thinking back to those days. Last night, I was with a few of my poker friends who've been coming around for haircuts for a lot of years. Most of them remember Tony.

"We got to talking, and one of them remembered something I'd forgotten. If you're looking for a person close to Tony who had a habit of straying, you might want to talk to his sister-in-law, Lee Romano. In the first couple of years after she and Emil were married, we heard rumours that Lee was cheating on Emil. Now, I can't say if it's true. But we all heard the rumours. However, if she was straying, she must have stopped because the rumours died out."

"Were there any rumours about her and Tony?"

"I'm not sure. I don't think Tony would have encouraged her, but you never know, do you? And you never know who might have said something to Emil, either."

"Thanks for passing this on."

Lee Romano had a puzzled look on her face when she came to the door of her house. "Yes? What is it now?"

Manziuk said, "Mrs. Romano, we—"

"Lee, please, Inspector."

"All right. Lee, we have a few more questions we'd like to ask you."

She seemed reluctant to open the door this time, but she did. Then she led the way into her living room and asked them to be seated. But she didn't offer any refreshments. Just sat on the edge of a chair across from them and waited as if she was in a hurry to leave.

Ryan said, "Lee, in order to find out what happened to Tony, we have to dig into the past. Sometimes that means dredging up memories of painful topics."

"Yes, I understand that. But what does this have to do with me?"

"At the time of Tony's death, you were already married to Emil, right?"

"We were married roughly two years before then."

"Was your marriage a happy one?"

"Yes, it was."

"You continued to work?"

"I graduated as an RN shortly before I got married, so naturally I wanted to work. I enjoyed what I did. And, of course, the money didn't hurt."

"You had no children?"

"We've never had children."

"Was that by choice?"

"I don't see what our having children or not has to do with Tony's death, but since I'm not embarrassed by it, I'll answer. It wasn't our choice to begin with, but when I didn't get pregnant and the doctors told me we'd have to use in vitro fertilization, we decided we were both fine without kids. We could always borrow Felicia and Bruno if we needed a fix."

"Do you have any regrets?" Ryan asked.

Lee pushed her hair back. "Oh, now and then, I suppose. But not really. I love what I do, and Emil is happy with his hardware store, his sports, and watching TV in his spare time."

"You could have adopted."

She shrugged. "I suppose."

Lee looked at Manziuk. "Is this really getting you any-where?"

"We're trying to get a sense of who you are and what's important to you," he said.

"Well, not all women have to have children to be content. I've been able to help hundreds if not thousands of people through my job as a nurse. I couldn't have done as much if I'd had children of my own to look after, too."

"I guess," Ryan said, "what we really want to know is if perhaps you might have been bored early on in your marriage and looked elsewhere."

Lee stared at her. "You're seriously asking me that?"

Ryan stared back. "Yes."

"You mean Tony, don't you? You want to know if I was having an affair with Tony."

"Yes, we do."

Lee laughed, then relaxed in the chair and stretched her legs out in front of her for a moment before leaning forward again. "I know it's not funny, but Tony was close to the last person on earth I'd have had an affair with."

"Why?" Ryan asked.

"Well, for starters, all he could talk about were Gina, his kids, and soccer. And he was one of my husband's best friends, never mind my brother-in-law, so that would be really gross. And you couldn't tell Tony something and ask him to keep it a secret. He'd just blurt it out the first chance he got. So if he was having an affair, everyone would know all about it within a day or two. And—well, I could go on and on. But, no. Never." She stood up. "And now, if you're done, I have some things I need to do today."

As Manziuk and Ryan headed to the front door, Lee said, "Sorry for the dead end, officers. You'll have to look for another rabbit hole to jump into."

SEVEN

They were on their way to the hardware store when Ryan's phone buzzed again. "It's Ford," she said. "He's found something." She put her phone on speaker.

"Technically, Kelly found something," Ford's voice said. "Because the crime scene was in a place we couldn't keep an eye on easily, we set up a couple of surveillance cameras at the parking lot nearest to the beginning of the trail that led to it. So I asked Kelly to take a look at the tapes and see if she could spot this Questioner person. Evan and Felicia told me the time when they saw him, and gave me a pretty good idea of his appearance. And Kelly found him pretty quickly. He drove a Jeep and had his bicycle in the trunk.

"Kelly decided on her own to keep looking at the video to see if she could spot whoever brought the chain. Now, because the crime scene is off the trails, the chain could have been dumped there at any time on the weekend without people noticing, but she thought at least it might give us some leads.

"There turned out to be a lot of cars. But, there was one car that kind of stood out. It came in really early Sunday morning, at 5:05, and was driven out at 6:17."

"Can you see the person well enough to identify him?"

"No, but we think it's a woman. She's wearing a black jacket and a floppy hat that covers her face."

"So you can't see her face at all?"

"No. The hat is really floppy and she has her back to the camera."

"But you think it's a woman?"

"I'd say we're ninety percent certain, just from the overall shape. But it could possibly be a slim man."

"What kind of car?"

"A light-coloured Honda Accord. Silver would be my guess, but maybe white, grey, or taupe.

"Does anyone on our list have a Honda Accord?"

"Yes, someone does." Ford paused for effect. "And the licence plate number matches, too."

"You got the number?"

"We did. Not to mention that of the person who calls himself the Questioner."

"Way to go!" Ryan yelled.

"Okay, you've got our full attention," Manziuk said. "Who was it?"

"Lee Romano."

Manziuk swore. "We just left her."

"Well, you might want to go back."

As he made a quick right turn to go around a block, Manziuk said, "On our way."

"What about the Questioner?" Ryan asked.

"A poet, if you can believe. He teaches workshops on writing, too. No record. It seems he got bored with writing poetry nobody knows about and decided to get an audience this way. Benson and I are going to visit him today.

"But that's not all we have," Ford chuckled. "Remember the tiny white speck we found on the link that joined the cross to the chain? We've identified it. It's Super Lube Synthetic Grease. It's a heavy duty lubricant that protects against friction, wear, rust, and corrosion. And it didn't exist seventeen years ago."

"So, where might the chain have been to come into contact with this grease?"

"A garage, a workroom…"

"What about a hardware store?" Ryan asked. "One that does maintenance for bikes?"

Lee had changed into a flared pink skirt and a lacy white blouse and used a red scarf to tie her hair back into a ponytail. To Manziuk, she brought back memories of the TV show *Happy Days*. When she saw who had rung her doorbell, she stood still for a moment, her mouth open. Finally, she said, "Did you forget something?"

"Yes," Ryan said, "we realized we had one more question. Why did you leave Tony's crucifix in the woods on Sunday morning?"

"What are you talking about?"

Manziuk moved up beside Ryan and Lee dropped back. "We have indisputable proof that you were at the woods early on Sunday morning. Now, you can answer here or we can take you down to police headquarters."

"Or I can call a lawyer."

"That's only necessary if you did something illegal."

"Did you?" Ryan asked.

"What is this proof you have that I did something with this—what did you say—crucifix?"

"Videotape showing your car, your licence plate, and you getting out and walking toward the trail that led to the crime scene." Ryan cocked her head on the side. "Give it up, Lee. We know it was you. We just want to know where you got the chain and why you took it to the woods."

Lee put her hands up to touch the scarf in her hair before moving back. "I suppose you might as well come in."

Ryan shut the front door and the three stood in the hallway. Lee leaned back against the wall near the stairs and crossed her arms.

"Where did you get the crucifix?" Manziuk asked.

"I—I found it."

"Where? When?"

"I don't remember."

"Let's go back to our original question," Ryan said. "Were you and Tony De Luca having an affair?"

Lee looked up. "No. Absolutely not." Her voice was firm.

"So where did you get his crucifix?"

"I—I lied. I did see Tony that night. He came over here after he finished work. It was just supposed to be for a few minutes. He was helping me do something to surprise Emil. But he fell off a ladder and hit his head, and died on impact. I'm a nurse. I did everything that could have been done, but it was no good. I knew nobody would believe what had really happened, so I carried his body to my car and took him to the woods and buried him. I—I was afraid."

"The crucifix?" Ryan asked.

"I couldn't bury it. I knew it was important to him and to his mother, and I didn't want it to be lost."

"Why didn't you give it to his family?"

"I wanted to, but how could I?"

"Why did you take it to the woods yesterday?"

"So that it could be found and his family would have it."

Manziuk said, "Or so that if we searched your home, it wouldn't be found?"

She hung her head. "Yes, that, too."

"Do you ride a bike?" Manziuk asked.

"A bike? No."

"Does Emil?"

"No. He used to, but he doesn't any more."

"Does Emil repair bikes at home?"

"Why would he do that when he has everything set up at the store?"

Ryan took over again. "Where did you really find the chain? In the hardware store?"

"What are you talking about? I had it here. In an old box in the back of my closet."

"Can you show us where it was kept?"

"I threw the box away. You can see my closet if you want."

"What was Tony doing when he fell?" Manziuk asked.

"I'd bought a new light for the hallway here—to go above the stairs. I wanted to surprise Emil when he came home."

"Didn't Emil usually come home shortly after nine on Friday nights?"

"He often worked late. Or stopped at a pub on the way."

"But you had no way of knowing that Emil would stay out late, did you?"

"I think he told me he'd be late."

"When did you arrange for Tony to come here after work on Friday?"

"Um—I stopped by and talked to him at the barber shop."

Ryan said, "Raphael didn't say anything about your stopping by."

"Maybe I phoned."

"We can check the phone records."

"Where did Tony hit his head when he fell off the ladder?" Manziuk asked.

"I—um—there." She pointed to the square post at the end of the stair railing. "He hit his head on the edge of it."

"You know we have a forensic team who can match the damage in his skull to the post, right?"

"I think maybe we had a different post then."

"How did you get his body from your car to the woods?"

"I carried it. I'm a nurse. I'm strong. I slung it over my back."

"And you also carried a shovel?"

Lee looked down. "I made two trips. I took his body in first and then I went back for the shovel."

"Lee, I don't believe any of this," Manziuk said. "Where in the hardware store did you really find the chain?"

"I told you," she whispered as she sank onto the stairs. "I had it here. It wasn't at the hardware store."

"Emil killed him, didn't he?" Ryan said. "Did he tell you or did you figure it out when you found the chain where he hid it at the store?"

Lee put her face in her hands and began to sob.

Some minutes later, Lee led them to the kitchen, where she poured herself a glass of wine before sitting at the table. "It was all my fault," she said. "You were right. I was having an affair back then, but not with Tony. One of the doctors I worked with at the hospital was—well, let's just say I learned later that he had quite a reputation among the staff. He was very interested in me, and I was young and not well-versed in the ways of the world. I guess you'd say he seduced me, but in such a way that I felt honoured to be the object of his affections. I began to think Emil and I had nothing in common—I mean, all he was interested in was the hardware store and watching sports! I began to think I'd been a fool to marry him. And this doctor fed into that. I'd have left Emil in a second if the doctor had suggested it."

"Did Emil know?" Manziuk asked.

"I didn't think so. But then one day, he said something to me. Nothing direct, just a sort of, 'You seem to be late coming home a lot' kind of thing. And I said something lame. I don't remember his words, but I remember the look he gave me. It woke me up. I realized that if I continued seeing the doctor I'd destroy my marriage, and I didn't want that to happen. I loved Emil. That epiphany happened just a few days before Tony disappeared."

Ryan asked, "So, where did you find the chain?"

She took a deep breath and slowly expelled it. "At the hardware store. It was in a small box hidden in the back corner of the lowest shelf in the back room. There was a bunch of junk in front of it. I'd never have found it except I was in the mood to clean the back room, for the first time in years, so I was taking everything out and cleaning the shelves and throwing out or reorganizing things."

"When was this?"

"About two years after Tony disappeared. I think it might have been part of my mission to prove to Emil that I was a good wife."

"Did you tell Emil you'd found the chain?"

She shook her head. "How could I? I realized at once what had happened. And I knew it had been an accident. Emil can be kind of gruff, but he would never intentionally hurt anyone."

"So what did you do?"

"I put the chain back exactly the way it had been, and I put everything else on that shelf back the way it had been, too."

There was a long silence, which Lee broke. "You asked me about having children. Well, how could I bring a child into this world knowing that its father might be arrested at any time?"

Manziuk asked, "Why did you take the chain to the crime scene area yesterday?"

"I was afraid that you'd search the hardware store and find it. But I couldn't just throw it away. I thought—I hoped—if I took it to the place where his body was found, you'd think the searchers had missed it before."

"So you've never said anything to Emil about it?"

"What could I say? If Emil thought Tony and I were having an affair, it was all my fault." She shook her head. "And now this is my fault too. If I hadn't panicked and taken the chain to the woods, you'd never have found out."

"Don't blame yourself," Manziuk said. "It was only a matter of time. We were actually on our way to talk to Emil when we found out about the video."

Lee shivered. "What are you going to do now?"

"I have one more question," Ryan said. "What were you really doing the night Tony disappeared?"

"Emil had told me he'd be late, so after my shift ended and I filled out my reports, I met my doctor friend for dinner. I got back here around ten-thirty. Emil wasn't home yet."

"Okay," Manziuk said. "We're going to have someone stay here with you while we go and talk to your husband."

"You don't want me to warn him."

"That," Ryan said, "and we have to decide whether or not to arrest you for obstructing justice and aiding and abetting a murderer."

Lee put her hands to her face and fell back on the couch in tears.

Joe Romano was in the front of the hardware store talking to a customer when Manziuk and Ryan entered.

"Emil?" Manziuk said.

Joe motioned toward the back room.

Emil looked up in apparent surprise when they came through the door. He finished putting a new tire on a Diamondback racing bike and then stood up. "Yes? Something I can do for you?"

"We have a few more questions," Ryan said.

"Okay. What are they?"

"Why did you kill Tony De Luca? And was it an accident or intentional?"

Emil scowled. "I did not kill Tony. Neither by accident nor by intent. And I wish you'd give up thinking you're going to somehow trap me into saying I did."

"What if we told you that your wife has confessed to killing him?" Manziuk said.

"I don't think that's very funny."

"I can play her taped confession if you like," Ryan said.

"That's ridiculous. Where is she?"

"Do you want to tell us what you were really doing that Friday night? We know you didn't get the bikes fixed that you said you were working on. Not until the next week."

Emil hit the wall next to him. "All right. Yes, I can tell you where I was. I left here early to spy on Lee. When she left the hospital after her shift was over, I followed her to a restaurant, where she met with one of the doctors she worked with. And afterward, I followed him to his house and told him that if I ever caught him with Lee again, I'd file for divorce and charge him with alienation of affections. And I'd do a few other things, too. Then I drove home, but when I saw Lee's car in the driveway and the light on in the bedroom, I decided to go to a pub and have a few drinks before going in. I was afraid if Lee was still awake, I might say something I'd regret."

"Did you expect her to meet with the doctor?"

"No. I'd thought for some time that she was messing around with somebody, but I had no idea who it was."

"Did you think it might have been Tony?"

"I did for a while."

"Why?"

"The way they'd joke sometimes. Kind of flirting. At least, I thought it was. And I heard a rumour."

"So if you didn't kill Tony, why did you hide Tony's crucifix on the shelf here?"

"What the—? I have no idea what you're talking about."

"Tony's crucifix. The one Lee took out to the woods yesterday and left for us to find in the hope that we'd think we'd missed it when we searched the area earlier."

Emil stared at Ryan. "Lee had Tony's crucifix?"

"You hid it here and she found it."

"I have no idea what you're talking about. Do you have proof of any of this?"

"We have the chain and the cross. It's been identified as Tony's. We have video proof as well as Lee's admission that she took it to the wooded area."

"And she told you she found it here?"

"That's what she told us, and we believe her. She found the chain a couple of years after Tony disappeared and she kept quiet in order to protect you."

"But that's ridic—I didn't—I had no idea the chain was here. Where was it?"

"I'll tell you where it was." Joe came into the room. "I put the 'Closed' sign up."

"Mr. Romero," Manziuk said, "was it you who hid the crucifix?"

"Yes."

"Where did you hide it?"

Joe motioned to the bottom shelf. "There. In the far corner. In a little box."

"Do you want to tell us what happened?" Ryan asked.

"Dad," Emil said, "maybe we should call a lawyer."

"It's okay." Joe sat down on an old chair that was covered with many colours of paint. "I've been wanting to get this off my chest ever since they found him."

"Take your time," Manziuk said. "What happened that Friday night?"

"I was waiting for Tony when he came out of the barber shop, and we walked down the street. He told me he was supposed to meet Dom for drinks, but we just kept talking and walking, and ended up at his house. We were in front of his house when I accused him of cheating on my daughter with Lee. He denied it, but I didn't believe him.

"When we realized we were in front of their house, Tony persuaded me to cross the street to the park so we could keep talking without anybody hearing us. I didn't want to, but he started across the street, so I followed.

"We stopped near some trees, where we thought nobody'd be able to see or hear us. I didn't believe anything he said, and finally I told him I was going in the house to tell Gina right that minute. He grabbed my arm to stop me, but I pushed him away, and he lost his footing and went flying backward."

Tears began streaming down Joe's face.

"Was he knocked out?" Manziuk asked.

"For a minute or two. He'd hit the side of his head on a small concrete barrier. But he got up okay, although there was blood streaming down from the cut.

"I felt terrible. I never intended to hurt him. I told you earlier, I'd never hurt anyone on purpose. It was just terrible luck that he landed on the concrete. He could just as easily have landed on grass and been none the worse for it."

"What happened next?" Ryan asked.

"I helped him up, but after he got back on his feet, he talked kind of funny. Like he wanted nothing more than to fight me. I started to walk away, but out of the corner of my eye I saw he was going to take a swing at me.

"I ducked, and he nearly lost his balance. And then he came at me again. I pushed him—but I was only trying to keep him from hitting me, not wanting to hurt him. I was worried about him. But all of a sudden, he went limp and fell straight back and hit his head on the concrete and he—he died instantly. One second he was alive, trying to knock my head off, and the next second he was as limp and lifeless as a rag doll."

Emil interrupted. "Dad, why didn't you call for help?"

Joe shook his head. "I checked his pulse. He wasn't breathing. His head had stopped bleeding. I knew he was dead. And then I panicked. I was certain that no one would believe it was an accident. Especially anyone who'd known my parents and what growing up was like with them always fighting. I was certain everyone would say I did it on purpose and I didn't. I swear I didn't."

Manziuk asked, "What did you do after you were positive he was dead?"

"I decided I had to hide him. So I dragged his body back into some bushes. My house is a few blocks down a back lane that comes out at one end of the park, so I went down the lane and got my truck and a wheelbarrow. Then I drove back to the park and got as close as I could to the body, and used the wheelbarrow to get it to the truck.

"I wanted to take him as far away from where we lived as possible, so I decided to bury him in the Don Valley. I'd been out there a number of times because I had a customer in that area who'd ordered a few things from me, and I'd delivered them."

"But why bury him?" Emil asked. "Why not leave his body to be found?"

"The more I thought about it, the more I realized that while it was going to be horrible for my daughter to lose her husband, it would be twice as bad if she lost her father too. She'd already lost her mother way too young. I wanted to be here to help her and the kids. If his body was found, then the police might find out the truth."

"What did you do after you drove to the Don Valley?" Manziuk asked.

"I used the wheelbarrow to move his body, and I went far into the woods so it wouldn't be easy to find. I dug a grave about three or four feet deep—the ground started to get really hard and rocky about then—and I put him in. I—I saw his crucifix and I had to remove it. And I remembered to take his wallet to make it look like a robbery if they did find him. Then I did my best to have a funeral service for him."

"What did you do with his wallet?"

"I burned the cards from his wallet and threw it in the garbage. I gave the money that was in it to a homeless man."

"And the chain?"

"I—I couldn't bury it. I knew how much it meant to him and to his parents. But I couldn't give it to them. So I hid it. I thought that, after I died, Emil would find it and see that Gina got it."

Emil had been listening in disbelief. "Dad, I still don't understand. Why did you confront Tony in the first place?"

"Because there was a lot of talk about Lee from the men I knew. They were joking about her. I didn't want you to know. I didn't want you to be hurt."

"But who told you she was seeing Tony?"

"A couple of them had been in the barber shop when Lee came in to see Tony, and she gave him a big hug and a kiss before she left."

"When was that?"

"A week or so before."

Emil hit his head with his hand. "Dad, I heard the exact same story! Afterwards, I asked Lee about it. She said one of her patients in the hospital had found out she was related to Tony and asked her to give him a hug and a kiss for her. She was a single mom, and he'd coached her son in soccer, and the kid had gone from being a major problem to being a model kid." Emil sighed. "You were right, Dad. Lee was seeing somebody. But it was a doctor. Not Tony. Never Tony."

Joe's face crumpled. "I thought—I was only trying to help—to look after you and Gina."

Emil put his arm around his father. "It's okay, Dad. I understand. It was an accident. Tony would forgive you. Gina will, too."

After a few minutes, Joe turned to Manziuk. "Seventeen years is too long a time to keep a secret like this to yourself. I'm tired of pretending. I'd like to go with you now."

"I'll get you a lawyer, Dad," Emil said.

"It's okay, son. I'll be fine. Believe it or not, I feel kinda relieved."

Manziuk and Ryan left the store with Joe walking between them, leaving Emil standing by himself staring after them.

Back at police headquarters, Ryan and Manziuk had a conference call with Dr. Wong and Dr. Weaver and the four of them discussed Joe's statement.

"Yes," Dr. Wong said, "that would account for everything I saw."

"I agree," Dr. Weaver said.

Ryan said, "What about what he said about Tony's getting up and lunging at him after he'd been unconscious for a minute or so? Is that even possible? Would he have been able to do that if he had a concussion?"

"Yes," Dr. Weaver said, "it's entirely possible. Especially if he first hit the side of his head near the front, which is what it sounds like happened. Each part of the brain controls different things, so the reaction depends entirely on which part of the brain is damaged. Aggression is actually one symptom of a concussion. He could have struck out blindly, not even realizing what he was doing."

"What will you charge him with?" Dr. Wong asked.

Manziuk answered. "We're leaning toward manslaughter. I don't believe it was premeditated. There's also failure to report a death and unlawful disposal of a dead body. He could get up to five years just for that."

"And Lee?"

"I'm convinced she believed it was her husband who was guilty. A good lawyer could argue that she had a wife's right not to incriminate him."

After they hung up, Ryan said, "Usually, I'm more than happy to see somebody get the punishment they deserve, but this is different. They're all essentially nice people, but because they listened to gossip, kept secrets, and jumped to wrong conclusions, they totally messed up their lives."

"I think they'll be able to plea bargain down, but you're right. Too many poor decisions."

"And too little communication," Ryan said.

"Yes."

When Paul Manziuk got home that night, Mike was in the kitchen building a six-layer sandwich. Paul stopped in the doorway to watch. "You really think you can eat all that?"

"Absolutely! I expended a lot of energy this weekend."

"I didn't see you last night. How was the tournament?"

"Great! We didn't win, but we made the finals. Lost fifteen to twelve, so we're getting better. Next time, who knows?"

"You did well?"

"Yeah, I got four goals and three assists."

"Great!"

As Mike sat down at the table, Paul said, "You wanted to ask me something the other morning. I'm sorry I had to leave in such a hurry."

"How's your case going?"

"We've solved it."

"Great!"

"So, what did you want to ask me?"

"Hmm. Let me think." Mike took a bite of his sandwich and chewed thoughtfully.

Paul went to the refrigerator and found the plate Loretta had left for him. He put it in the microwave and hit reheat, then stood waiting.

Mike worked on his sandwich. "Oh, I remember what I wanted to ask you."

The microwave dinged and Paul took his plate over to the table, then got a fork and sat down across from his son. "Yes? What is it?"

"Well, this is my last year of school, so I'm going to need to decide what I want to do next year."

"Right."

"So, here's what I'm thinking. I don't have any idea what I really want to do, but I have a lot of different interests. So I had thought maybe you and I could go over the things I like and kind of try to fit them into areas I could check out. But you were busy, so this afternoon, I made an appointment with a guidance counsellor. We're getting together on Wednesday."

Blast! Paul thought to himself. *I blew another one.* But he said, "I think that's a terrific idea." After a moment, he added, "Maybe we can go over it together afterwards?"

"Sure. That'll be great."

Jacquie Ryan walked into the kitchen and found her family sitting around the table eating but not saying much to each other.

She went up to her room to get rid of her gun and change her clothes, and then came back to the table, where she took a seat and ate the food Grams had prepared. But when Precious started to leave the table, Jacquie said, "Hold it."

"What do you mean, 'Hold it'?"

"You're not going any place until Grams tells us why she doesn't want to change up the kitchen."

Precious opened her mouth to argue, but her mother said, "Sit down, child." She sat down.

"Well, Grams?" Jacquie said. "What's so important to you about this kitchen? It's old and it's inconvenient and it might not even be safe. But you don't want to change it, and you're a smart lady. So you have to have a good reason."

Her grandmother's eyes were welling up with tears.

"Jacquie's right, Mom," Vida said. "What is it we're missing?"

After a long moment, the older woman said, "When we bought this house, it was in pretty bad shape. Over the years, we fixed it up as best we could. But we couldn't afford to hire people to do it. So we did as much as we could ourselves. My Benny—your dad—he laid the flooring. And he made those cupboards all by himself. What you see as old and ugly, I see as the best efforts of a man who loved his family."

"Oh, Mama!" Vida and Noelle both got up and went to hug their mother.

Precious had tears in her eyes, too, as she leaned over to kiss her grandmother's cheek. "I'm so sorry, Grams. I didn't realize."

"I know it needs fixing," Grams said, "but it's so hard for me. Especially when you talk about it as if it's something ugly. All I see here is beauty. And love."

Jacquie got up and joined her family as they embraced and remembered the man who had been husband, father, and grandfather. "We'll work it out," she said. "When we're all ready, and the time is right, we'll do it together. Plus, when we do it, we'll figure out a way to keep some of the things Grampa built. And the things you made, too."

Two days later, Felicia Marino walked through the doors of the veterinary clinic where Evan worked and asked the receptionist if she could speak to him. A few minutes later, he came out of the back.

He was smiling. "He's got a clean bill of health."

"Yes!"

"Can I see him?"

"Sure. Come with me."

Felicia followed him into a back room where the little dog was sitting in a kennel looking out. His fur was now light brown instead of a dull brownish grey, his ears were pricked up, and his eyes were bright. He barked a greeting to her, his tail wagging in ecstasy.

"Hi, Buddy," she said as she knelt down.

Evan opened the kennel and the dog bolted into Felicia's outstretched arms.

"So, we found his owner," Evan said.

Felicia looked up. "You did?

"Well, technically, his owner found us. Because of the article Special Constable Benson put out with the picture of him after his bath."

"And?"

"Apparently, the lady got him from a friend of hers whose dog had an unexpected litter of pups about six weeks after escaping from the yard overnight. The lady got him at eight weeks, and was finding him a bit of a problem. She works full time, and the dog was getting bored and chewing up slippers and chair legs and so forth. She was trying various things to wear him out, but one day when she took him for a long walk, he managed to slip out of his collar and run off. She says she chased after him, but he was too fast for her. And that's the last she saw of him.

"She says she tried to find him, and she put up some posters in the area, but it was pretty clear to me she really didn't want him back. When I offered to take him off her hands, she was delighted."

Felicia pumped her fist in the air. "Yes!"

"Are you sure your parents are going to be okay with your keeping him?"

She got to her feet, Buddy in her arms. "They are. Mom isn't at all happy about it, but Dom told her we owe the dog a lot and she agreed. And Papa De Luca is going to look after him during the day when I have classes. I think he's looking forward to the company. My younger brothers are thrilled, of course. Bruno too, although he won't admit it."

"Okay, let's get him ready. I've got a collar and a leash for you, and some food we recommend, and dishes. And some bags for cleanup. And a couple of toys. Oh, and a bed. And a crate for him to sleep in, and to stay in when you all go out, at least for now, so he doesn't get into too much trouble."

"Wait! You're giving me all that?"

"It's my way of getting on your mother's good side after foisting an unwanted dog on her."

Felicia tilted her head. "So you've decided you want to be on her good side, have you?"

"Well, I plan to be hanging around your family quite a bit. For many years to come, actually."

Felicia grinned.

As Evan put a collar on Buddy, he became serious. "How is your family doing, anyway?"

"Pretty good. Everybody's been crying a lot, of course. But Grandpa Romero seems to be relieved that it's all come out, and his lawyer thinks he'll be able to get him off with a light sentence. I hope so.

"It's weird, but Emil and Lee are happier than I've ever seen them. They're even talking about adopting a couple of older kids who need a home.

"And Mom and Dom—well, they're sad at how it turned out, but I think they're mostly relieved to know that it really was just a terrible accident and not something worse. Papa was pretty angry that Grandpa Joe kept it a secret. Said he'd have nothing more to do with him. Called him all sorts of names. But then he started crying and said they'd been friends all those years and family for more than twenty years, so he guessed he'd have to ask God to help him find a way to forgive Joe. Said that's what Mama would want."

Evan nodded. "Bitterness just eats at you. And I can see why Joe didn't say anything. The police might not have believed him. So many things went wrong."

"And now, because of you and Buddy, they've been put right. It might be crazy, but I think the timing—it's so weird! I don't know if it was God or Daddy or fate or luck that made Buddy run away so you could spot him that first day, and find my dad. And then for us to meet that morning…"

"I don't know for sure," Evan said, "but I'm not a big believer in blind chance or luck. I think we were meant to meet someday, and this turned out to be the way."

Buddy starting squirming, and Felicia set him down.

Evan put the leash on him and Felicia started out, carrying the bed and letting Buddy lead her. Evan followed with the rest of the supplies.

"So you're coming for supper tonight?" Felicia asked through the open car window when she was ready to leave. Buddy was lying in his new kennel in the back seat, chewing on a stuffed toy.

"I am. Assuming you still want me."

"You realize my family will all be there, and they'll ask you a million questions?"

"I'm prepared. If I run out of answers, I'll just look at you with big sad eyes the way Buddy does."

Felicia laughed and put the car in drive. "I promise to come to the rescue."

Acknowledgements

All over the world, people go missing every single day.

For a couple of years, I've been thinking about how many people go missing every day in the Greater Toronto area, where I live. One of the reasons I know this is because I follow both the Toronto and York Region police on Twitter. On a regular basis, they post photos and information about where someone was seen. Sometimes it's an older person who has dementia or Alzheimer's; sometimes a young child who has wandered away; often a young person or a middle-aged person who has chosen to leave home; but sometimes it's a person who has become a statistic because of an accident or another individual.

Most of the missing people are eventually found. And thanks to social media, it can be quite fast these days. But every now and then, the person is never heard from again, or turns up as what is generally termed "human remains."

Writing this story is my way of drawing attention to that reality, as well as my attempt to understand the pain of those who are left behind, possibly never knowing what happened to their loved ones.

My son Daniel, who is a veterinarian, helped me with the details about the stray dog. Any mistakes are mine.

I've used Google to check on so many things for this book, from what happens to items buried in the ground to information about missing persons.

Thanks to my husband Les, who is always my first reader; to Audrey Dorsch for copy-editing, and to my beta readers Patricia Anne Elford, Janet Sketchley, Ann Brent, and Theresa Goldrick for finding pesky glitches. Thanks also to a number of my readers for occasional encouraging words that keep me writing.

J. A. Menzies

While I'd hate to stumble on a real body under any circumstances, I have a thing about noticing the "perfect" locations for finding mythical bodies. In order not to waste this fascinating (and hopefully, unusual) skill, I decided to write mysteries.

Truth is, I've been reading mysteries since I first discovered Trixie Beldon (I owned every book). Later, I discovered and devoured the work of Erle Stanley Gardner, John Creasey, Agatha Christie, Georgette Heyer, Ngaio Marsh, Dorothy L. Sayers, Desmond Bagley, Raymond Chandler, Emma Lathen, Marjorie Allingham, and others far too numerous to list here.

I still go back and reread many of the authors of the British Golden Age—they're my comfort-books. I also read a wide variety of contemporary authors.

I'm a member of various writers' organizations, including Sisters in Crime and Crime Writers of Canada. I also teach workshops for writers. I especially enjoy sharing some of my secrets on developing plots. (One of my favorite reviews, from *Library Journal*, called me a "master of plotting.")

CONNECT WITH ME AT:

http://jamenzies.com

SHADED LIGHT

THE CASE OF THE TACTLESS TROPHY WIFE

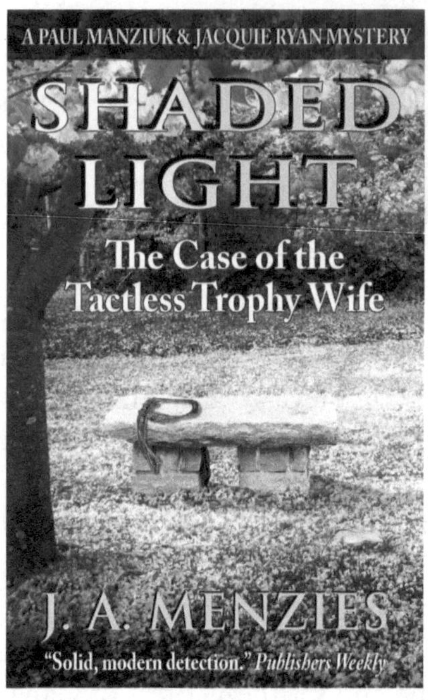

The first in a classic police procedural series of traditional whodunits set in contemporary Toronto.

A weekend house party at a Toronto lawyer's estate. A young woman's body in the garden. Enter homicide detectives Paul Manziuk and Jacquie Ryan for their first case together. "He's white, an abrupt, patronizing veteran, while she's a recently promoted, vivacious black woman—but… the two rub elbows and tempers to captivating effect." *Publishers Weekly.*

GLITTER OF DIAMONDS

THE CASE OF THE RECKLESS RADIO HOST

The second in a classic police procedural series of traditional whodunits set in contemporary Toronto.

When a star player on the local baseball team has a tantrum after a loss, the Toronto media reacts quickly. A female radio talk-show host even asks for a volunteer to knock some sense into him with a baseball bat. Soon, homicide detectives Paul Manziuk and Jacquie Ryan scramble to catch the murderer before he or she strikes again.

SHADOW OF A BUTTERFLY

THE CASE OF THE HARMLESS OLD WOMAN

The third in a classic police procedural series of traditional whodunits set in contemporary Toronto.

When an elderly woman is murdered in the common room of the penthouse floor of a luxury Toronto high-rise that caters to famous seniors, residents and staff suspect a deluded mercy-killer. As homicide detectives Paul Manziuk and Jacqueline Ryan follow rabbit-trails, sorting through half-truths and long-buried secrets, they realize they're missing something; but what?

7 SHORT STORIES

INCLUDING PAUL MANZIUK & JACQUIE RYAN IN "THE CASE OF THE SNEEZING ACCOUNTANT"

Includes personal notes by the author
on the writing of each story.

A wife who murders her cheating husband, a knife-wielder
foiled by an unexpected sneeze, a dying woman with a
deadly secret that changed lives, an old man trying to make
up for his past... These stories run the gamut of crime-
writing and will keep you guessing to the last word.

How to Make an Author Happy

Writing a book is a lot of work.
Writing a **good** book is even more work.

If you like this book and would like to show your appreciation for the effort I put into writing it (thus encouraging me to write more books), here are 4 ways to do it.

1. Write a review. Post your review on bookstore sites, Goodreads, your blog, and/or anyplace else you frequent. It doesn't have to be long. A couple of sentences is enough. (Just remember not to give away the plot!) And do let me know about your review. Even if you said a few negative things, it's okay.

2. Tell other people about my books. Better yet, buy some books and give them to people you think would enjoy them too.

3. Buy my other books. Or get them from your library. If you liked this one, you'll likely enjoy the others too.

4. Connect with me by signing up for my reader updates, following on Twitter and/or FaceBook, etc.

Trust me, I'll appreciate it very much. The world of a writer can be a lonely one.

Wondering where to find me?

Sign up for my email reader updates at:

jamenzies.com

PUBLISHER

MurderWillOut Mysteries publishes whodunits set in Canada but written in the classic Golden Age style. It's an imprint of That's Life! Communications, a niche Canadian publisher.

murderwillout.com